John Henry Newman

Stray essays on controversial points

Variously illustrated

John Henry Newman

Stray essays on controversial points
Variously illustrated

ISBN/EAN: 9783337281670

Printed in Europe, USA, Canada, Australia, Japan

Cover: Foto ©Andreas Hilbeck / pixelio.de

More available books at **www.hansebooks.com**

STRAY ESSAYS

ON CONTROVERSIAL POINTS,

VARIOUSLY ILLUSTRATED:

BY

CARDINAL NEWMAN.

CONTENTS.

ESSAY I.

INSPIRATION IN ITS RELATION TO REVELATION.

ESSAY II.

FURTHER ILLUSTRATIONS.

ESSAY III.

REVELATION IN ITS RELATION TO FAITH.

ESSAY I.

ESSAY I.

INSPIRATION IN ITS RELATION TO REVELATION.

§ 1.

IT has lately been asked, what answer do we Catholics give to the allegation urged against us by men of the day, to the effect that we demand of our converts an assent to views and interpretations of Scripture which modern science and historical research have utterly discredited.

As this alleged obligation is confidently maintained against us, and with an array of instances in support of it, I think it should be either denied or defended; and the best mode perhaps of doing, whether the one or the other, will be, instead of merely dealing with the particular instances adduced in proof, to state what we really do hold as regards Holy Scripture, and what a Catholic is bound to believe. This I propose now to do, and in doing it, I beg it to be understood that my statements are simply my

B

own, and involve no responsibility of any one besides myself.

§ 2.

A recent work of M. Renan's is one of those publications which have suggested or occasioned this adverse criticism upon our intellectual position. That author's abandonment of Catholicism seems (according to a late article in a journal of high reputation) in no small measure to have come about by his study of the Biblical text, especially that of the Old Testament. "He explains," says the article, "that the Roman Catholic Church admits no compromise on questions of Biblical criticism and history" . . . even though "the Book of Judith is an historical impossibility. Hence the undoubted fact that the Roman Catholic Church . . . insists on its members believing . . . a great deal more in pure criticism and pure history than the strictest Protestants exact from their pupils or flocks." Should, then, a doubting Anglican contemplate becoming Catholic by way of attaining intellectual peace, "if his doubts turn on history and criticism, he will find the little finger of the Catholic Church thicker than the loins of Protestantism."

§ 3.

The serious question, then, which this article calls on us to consider, is, whether it is "an undoubted fact," as therein stated, that the Catholic Church does "insist" on her children's acceptance of certain Scripture informations on matters of fact in defiance of criticism and history. And my first duty on setting out is to determine the meaning of that vague word "insists," which I shall use in the only sense in which a Catholic can consent to use it.

I allow, then, that the Church, certainly, does "insist," when she speaks dogmatically, nay, or rather she more than insists, she obliges; she obliges us to an internal assent to that which she proposes to us. So far I admit, or rather maintain. And I admit that she obliges us in a most forcible and effective manner, that is, by the penalty of forfeiting communion with her, if we refuse our internal assent to her word. We cannot be real Catholics, if we do not from our heart accept the matters which she puts forward as divine and true. This is plain.

§ 4.

Next, to what does the Church oblige us? and what is her warrant for doing so? I answer: The matters which she can oblige us to accept with an internal assent are the matters contained in that Revelation of Truth, written or unwritten, which came to the world from our Lord and His Apostles; and this claim on our faith in her decisions as to the matter of that Revelation rests on her being the divinely-appointed representative of the Apostles, and the expounder of their words; so that whatever she categorically delivers about their formal acts, or their writings or their teaching, is an Apostolic deliverance. I repeat, the only sense in which the Church "insists" on any statement, Biblical or other, the only reason of her so insisting, is that that statement is part of the original Revelation, and therefore must be unconditionally accepted,—else, that Revelation is not, as a revelation, accepted at all.

The question then which I have to answer is: *What*, in matter of fact, has the Church (or the Pope), as the representative of God, said about Scripture, which, as being Apostolic, unerring Truth, is obligatory on our faith—that is, is *de fide*?

§ 5.

Many truths may be predicated about Scripture and its contents which are not obligatory on our faith, viz., such as are private conclusions from premisses, or are the *dicta* of theologians : such as about the author of the Book of Job, or the dates of St. Paul's Epistles. These are not obligatory upon us, because they are not the subjects of *ex cathedrâ* utterances of a General Council. Opinions of this sort may be true or not true, and lie open for acceptance or rejection, since no divine utterance has ever been granted to us about them, or is likely to be granted. We are not bound to believe what St. Jerome said or inferred about Scripture;

nor what St. Augustine, or St. Thomas, or Cardinal Caietan, or Fr. Perrone has said; but what the Church has enunciated, what the Councils, what the Pope, has determined. We are not bound to accept with an absolute faith what is not an Ecumenical dogma, or the equivalent of dogma (*vide infra*, § 17), that is, what is not *de fide*; such judgments, however powerfully enunciated, we may without loss of communion doubt, we may refuse to accept. This is what we must especially bear in mind, when we handle such objections as M. Renan's. We must not confuse what is indisputable as well as true, with what may indeed be true, yet is disputable. And this is to be received, not only as against M. Renan, but as against such criticisms as are to be met with in the publications of the day.

§ 6.

I must make one concession to him. In certain cases there may be a duty of silence, when there is no obligation of belief. Here no question of faith comes in. We will suppose that a novel opinion about Scripture or its contents is well grounded, and that a received opinion is open to doubt, in a case in which the Church has hitherto decided nothing, so that a new question needs a new answer: here, to profess the new opinion may be abstractedly permissible, but is not always permissible in practice. The novelty may be so startling as to require a full certainty that it is true; it may be so strange as to raise the question whether it will not unsettle ill-educated minds,—that is, though the statement is not an offence against faith, still it may be an offence against charity. It need not be heretical, yet at a particular time or place it may be so contrary to the prevalent opinion in the Catholic body, as in Galileo's case, that zeal for the supremacy of the Divine Word, deference to existing authorities, charity towards the weak and ignorant, and distrust of self, should keep a man from being impetuous or careless in circulating what nevertheless he holds to be true, and what, if indeed asked about, he cannot deny. The household of God has claims upon our tenderness in such matters which criticism and history have not.

§ 7.

For myself, I have no call or wish at all to write in behalf of such persons as think it a love of truth to have no "love of the brethren." I am indeed desirous of investigating for its own sake the limit of free thought consistently with the claims upon us of Holy Scripture; still, my especial interest in the inquiry is from my desire to assist those religious sons of the Church who are engaged in Biblical criticism and its attendant studies, and have a conscientious fear of transgressing the rule of faith; men who wish to ascertain how far their religion puts them under obligations and restrictions in their reasonings and inferences on such subjects,— what conclusions may, and what may not, be held without interfering with that internal assent which, if they would be Catholics, they are bound to give to the written Word of God. I do but contemplate the inward peace of religious Catholics in their own persons. Of course those who begin without belief in the religious aspect of the universe, are not likely to be brought to such belief by studying it merely on its secular side.

§ 8.

Here, then, the main question before us being what it is that a Catholic is free to hold about Scripture in general, or about its separate portions, or its statements, without compromising his firm inward assent to the dogmas of the Church, that is, to the *de fide* enunciations of Popes and Councils, we have first of all to inquire how many, and what, those dogmas are.

I answer that there are two such dogmas; one relates to the authority of Scripture, the other to its interpretation. As to the authority of Scripture, we hold it to be, in all matters of faith and morals, divinely inspired throughout; as to its interpretation, we hold that the Church is, in faith and morals, the one infallible expounder of that inspired text.

I begin with the question of its inspiration.

§ 9.

The books which constitute the canon of Scripture, or the Canonical books, are enumerated by the Tridentine Council, as we find them in the first page of our Catholic Bibles; and are in that Ecumenical Council's decree spoken of by implication as the work of inspired men. The Vatican Council speaks more distinctly, saying that the entire books, with all their parts, are divinely inspired, and adding an anathema upon impugners of this its definition.

There is another dogmatic phrase used by the Councils of Florence and Trent to denote the inspiration of Scripture, viz., "Deus *unus et idem* utriusque Testamenti Auctor." Since this left room for holding that by the word "Testamentum" was meant "Dispensation," as it seems to have meant in former Councils from the date of Irenæus, and as St. Paul uses the word in his Epistle to the Hebrews, the Vatican Council has expressly defined that the concrete *libri* themselves of the Old and New Testament "Deum habent Auctorem."

§ 10.

There is a further question, which is still left in some ambiguity, the meaning of the word "Auctor." "Auctor" is not identical with the English word "Author." Allowing that there are instances to be found in classical Latin in which "auctores" may be translated "authors," instances in which it even seems to mean "writers," it more naturally means "authorities." Its proper sense is "originator," "inventor," "founder," "primary cause;" (thus St. Paul speaks of our Lord as "Auctor salutis," "Auctor fidei;") on the other hand, that it was the inspired penmen who were the "writers" of their respective works seems asserted by St. John and St. Luke, and, I may say, in every paragraph of St. Paul's Epistles. In St. John we read, "This is the disciple who testifies of these things, and has *written* these things," and St. Luke says, "I have thought it good to *write* to thee," &c. However, if any one prefers to construe "auctor" as "author," or writer, let it be so—only, then there will be two writers of the Scriptures, the divine and the human.

§ 11.

And now comes the important question, in what respect are the Canonical books inspired? It cannot be in every respect, unless we are bound *de fide* to believe that "terra in æternum stat," and that heaven is above us, and that there are no antipodes. And it seems unworthy of Divine Greatness, that the Almighty should, in His revelation of Himself to us, undertake mere secular duties, and assume the office of a narrator, as such, or an historian, or geographer, except so far as the secular matters bear directly upon the revealed truth. The Councils of Trent

and the Vatican fulfil this anticipation; they tell
us distinctly the object and the promise of Scripture
inspiration. They specify "faith and moral conduct"
as the drift of that teaching which has the guarantee
of inspiration. What we need, and what is given
us, is not how to educate ourselves for this life;
we have abundant natural gifts for human society,
and for the advantages which it secures; but our
great want is how to demean ourselves in thought
and deed towards our Maker, and how to gain
reliable information on this urgent necessity.

§ 12.

Accordingly, four times does the Tridentine
Council insist upon "faith and morality" as the
scope of inspired teaching. It declares that the
"Gospel" is "the Fount of all *saving truth* and all
instruction in morals," that in the written books and
in the unwritten traditions, the Holy Spirit dictating,
this *truth* and *instruction* are contained. Then it
speaks of the books and traditions, "relating whether
to *faith* or to *morals*," and afterwards of "the con-
firmation of *dogmas* and establishment of *morals*."
Lastly, it warns the Christian people, "in matters
of *faith* and *morals*," against distorting Scripture
into a sense of their own.

In like manner the Vatican Council pronounces
that Supernatural Revelation consists "*in rebus
divinis*," and is *contained* "in libris scriptis et sine

scripto traditionibus;" and it also speaks of "petulantia ingenia" advancing wrong interpretations of Scripture "in rebus *fidei* et *morum* ad ædificationem *doctrinæ* Christianæ pertinentium."

§ 13.

But while the Councils, as has been shown, lay down so emphatically the inspiration of Scripture in respect to "faith and morals," it is remarkable that they do not say a word directly as to its inspiration in matters of fact. Yet are we therefore to conclude that the record of facts in Scripture does not come under the guarantee of its inspiration? we are not so to conclude, and for this plain reason:—the sacred narrative, carried on through so many ages, what is it but the very matter for our faith, and rule of our obedience? what but that narrative itself is the supernatural teaching, in order to which inspiration is given? What is the whole history, as it is traced out in Scripture from Genesis to Esdras, and thence on to the end of the Acts of the Apostles, what is it but a manifestation of Divine Providence, on the one hand interpretative (on a large scale and with analogical applications) of universal history, and on the other preparatory (typical and predictive) of the Evangelical Dispensation? Its pages breathe of providence and grace, of our Lord, and of His work and teaching, from beginning to end. It views facts in those relations in which neither ancients, such as the Greek and Latin classical historians, nor moderns, such as Niebuhr, Grote, Ewald, or Michelet, can view them. In this point of view it has God for its author, even though the finger of God traced no words but the Decalogue. Such is the claim of Bible history in its substantial fulness to be accepted *de fide* as true. In this point of view, Scripture is inspired, not only in faith and morals, but in all its parts which bear on faith, including matters of fact.

§ 14.

But what has been said leads to another serious question. It is easy to imagine a Code of Laws inspired, or a formal prophecy, or a Hymn, or a Creed, or a collection of Proverbs. Such works may be short, precise, and homogeneous; but inspiration on the one hand, and on the other a document, multiform and copious in its contents, as the Bible is, are at first sight incompatible ideas, and destructive of each other. How are we practically to combine the indubitable fact of a divine superintendence with the indubitable fact of a collection of such various writings?

§ 15.

Surely then, if the revelations and lessons in Scripture are addressed to us personally and practically, the presence among us of a formal judge and standing expositor of its words, is imperative. It is ante-cedently unreasonable to suppose that a book so complex, so unsystematic, in parts so obscure, the outcome of so many minds, times, and places, should be given us from above without the safeguard of some authority; as if it could possibly, from the nature of the case, interpret itself. Its inspiration does but guarantee its truth, not its interpretation. How are private readers satisfactorily to distinguish what is didactic and what is historical, what is fact and what is vision, what is allegorical and what is literal, what is idiomatic and what is grammatical, what is enunciated formally and what occurs *obiter*, what is only of temporary and what is of lasting obligation? Such is our natural anticipation, and it is only too exactly justified in the events of the last three centuries, in the many countries where private judgment on the text of Scripture has prevailed. The gift of inspiration requires as its complement the gift of infallibility.

Where then is this gift lodged, which is so neces-sary for the due use of the written word of God? Thus we are introduced to the second dogma in respect to Holy Scripture taught by the Catholic Religion. The first is that Scripture is inspired, the second, that the Church is the infallible inter-preter of that inspiration.

§ 16.

That the Church, and therefore the Pope, is that Interpreter is defined in the following words:—

First by the Council of Trent: " Nemo suâ prudentiâ innixus, in rebus fidei et morum ad ædificationem doctrinæ Christianæ pertinentium, Sacram Scripturam ad suos sensus contorquens, contra eum sensum quem tenuit et tenet Sancta Mater Ecclesia, cujus est judicare de vero sensu et interpretatione Scripturarum Sanctarum, aut etiam contra unanimem consensum Patrum, ipsam Scripturam Sacram interpretari audeat."

Secondly by the Council of the Vatican: "Nos, idem Decretum [Tridentinum] renovantes, hanc illius mentem esse declaramus, ut in rebus fidei et morum ad ædificationem doctrinæ Christianæ pertinentium, is pro vero sensu Sacræ Scripturæ habendus sit, quem tenuit et tenet Sancta Mater Ecclesia, cujus est judicare de vero sensu et interpretatione Scripturarum Sanctarum," &c.

§ 17.

Since, then, there is in the Church an authority, divinely appointed and plenary, for judgment and for appeal in questions of Scripture interpretation, in matters of faith and morals, therefore, by the very force of the words, there is one such authority, and only one.

Again, it follows hence, that, when the legitimate authority has spoken, to resist its interpretation is a sin against the faith, and an act of heresy.

And from this again it follows, that, till the Infallible Authority formally interprets a passage of Scripture, there is nothing heretical in advocating a contrary interpretation, provided of course there is nothing in the act intrinsically inconsistent with the faith, or the *pietas fidei*, nothing of contempt or rebellion, nothing temerarious, nothing offensive or scandalous, in the manner of acting or the circumstances of the case. I repeat, I am all along inquiring what Scripture, by reason of its literal text, obliges us to believe. An original view about Scripture or its parts may be as little contrary to the mind of the Church about it, as it need be an offence against its inspiration.

The proviso, however, or condition, which I have just made, must carefully be kept in mind. Doubtless, a certain interpretation of a doctrinal text may be so strongly supported by the Fathers, so continuous and universal, and so cognate and connatural with the Church's teaching, that it is virtually or practically as dogmatic as if it were a formal judgment delivered on appeal by the Holy See, and cannot be disputed except as the Church or Holy See opens its wording or its conditions. Hence the Vatican Council says, "Fide divinâ et Catholicâ ea omnia credenda sunt, quæ in verbo Dei scripto vel tradito continentur, vel ab Ecclesiâ sive solemni judicio, sive *ordinario* et *universali magisterio,* tanquam divinitus revelata, credenda proponuntur." And I repeat, that, though the Fathers were not inspired, yet their united testimony is of supreme authority; at the same time, since no Canon or List has been determined of the Fathers, the practical rule of duty is obedience to the voice of the Church.

§ 18.

Such then is the answer which I make to the main question which has led to my writing. I asked what obligation of duty lay upon the Catholic scholar or man of science as regards his critical treatment of the text and the matter of Holy Scripture. And now I say that it is his duty, first, never to forget that what he is handling is the Word of God, which, by reason of the difficulty of always drawing the line between what is human and what is divine, cannot be put on the level of other books, as it is now the fashion to do, but has the nature of a Sacrament, which is outward and inward, and a channel of supernatural grace; and secondly, that, in what he writes upon it, or its separate books, he is bound to submit himself internally, and to profess to submit himself, in all that relates to faith and morals, to the definite teaching of Holy Church.

This being laid down, let me go on to consider some of the critical distinctions and conclusions which are consistent with a faithful observance of these obligations.

§ 19.

Are the books or are the writers inspired? I answer, Both. The Council of Trent says the writers, " ab ipsis Apostolis, Spiritu Sancto dictante "; * the Vatican says the books, " si quis libros integros &c. divinitus inspiratos esse negaverit, anathema sit." Of course the Vatican decision is *de fide*, but it cannot annul the Tridentine. Both decrees are dogmatic truths. The Tridentine teaches us that the Divine Inspirer, inasmuch as He acted on the writer, acted, not immediately on the books themselves, but through the men who wrote them. The books are inspired, because the writers were inspired to write them. They are not inspired books, unless they came from inspired men.

There is one instance in Scripture of Divine Inspiration without a human medium: the Decalogue was written by the very finger of God. He wrote the Law upon the stone tables Himself. It has been thought that the Urim and Thummim was another instance of the immediate inspiration of a material substance; but anyhow such instances are exceptional; certainly, as regards Scripture, which

---

* I omit what is said about Tradition, as not coming into my subject.

C

alone concerns us here, there always have been two minds in the process of inspiration, a divine *Auctor*, and a human *Scriptor* ; and various important consequences follow from this appointment.

§ 20.

If there be at once a divine and a human mind co-operating in the formation of the sacred text, it is not surprising if there often be a double sense in that text, and (with obvious exceptions) never certain that there is not.

Thus Sara had her human and literal meaning in her words, "Cast out the bondwoman and her son," &c. ; but we know from St. Paul that those words were inspired by the Holy Ghost to convey a spiritual meaning. Abraham, too, on the Mount, when his son asked him whence was to come the victim for the sacrifice which his father was about to offer, answered "God will provide;" and he showed his own sense of his words afterwards, when he took the ram which was caught in the briers, and offered it as a holocaust. Yet those words were a solemn prophecy.

And is it extravagant to say, that, even in the case of men who have no pretension to be prophets or servants of God, He may by their means give us great maxims and lessons, which the speakers little thought they were delivering? as in the case of the Architriclinus in the marriage feast, who spoke of the bridegroom as having "kept the good wine until now;" words which it was needless for St. John to record, unless they had a mystical meaning.

Such instances raise the question whether the Scripture saints and prophets always understood the higher and divine sense of their words. As to Abraham, this will be answered in the affirmative; but I do not see reason for thinking that Sara was equally favoured. Nor is her case solitary; Caiphas, as high priest, spoke a divine truth by virtue of his office, little thinking of it, when he said that "one man must die for the people;" and St. Peter at Joppa at first did not see beyond a literal sense in his vision, though he knew that there was a higher sense, which in God's good time would be revealed to him.

And hence there is no difficulty in supposing that the Prophet Osee, though inspired, knew only his own literal sense of the words which he transmitted to posterity, "I have called my Son out of Egypt," the further prophetic meaning of them being declared by St. Matthew in his gospel. And such a divine sense would be both concurrent with, and confirmed by, that antecedent belief which prevailed among the Jews in St. Matthew's time, that their sacred books were in great measure typical, with an evangelical bearing, though as yet they might not know what those books contained in prospect.

§ 21.

Nor is it *de fide* (for that alone with a view to
Catholic Biblicists I am considering) that inspired
men, at the time when they speak from inspiration,
should always know that the Divine Spirit is visiting
them.

The Psalms are inspired; but, when David, in
the outpouring of his deep contrition, disburdened
himself before his God in the words of the *Miserere*,
could he, possibly, while uttering them, have been
directly conscious that every word he uttered was
not simply his, but another's? Did he not think
that he was personally asking forgiveness and
spiritual help? Doubt again seems incompatible
with a consciousness of being inspired. But Father
Patrizi, while reconciling two Evangelists in a passage
of their narratives, says, if I understand him rightly
(ii, p. 405), that though we admit that there were
some things about which inspired writers doubted,
this does not imply that inspiration allowed them
to state what is doubtful as certain, but only it
did not hinder them from stating things with a
doubt on their minds about them; but how can
the All-knowing Spirit doubt? or how can an
inspired man doubt, if he is conscious of his inspiration?

And again, how can a man whose hand is guided
by the Holy Spirit, and who knows it, make
apologies for his style of writing, as if deficient in

literary exactness and finish? If then the writer of Ecclesiasticus, at the very time that he wrote his Prologue, was not only inspired, but conscious of his inspiration, how could he have entreated his readers to "come with benevolence," and to make excuse for his "coming short in the composition of words"? Surely, if at the very time he wrote he had known it, he would, like other inspired men, have said, "Thus saith the Lord," or what was equivalent to it.

The same remark applies to the writer of the second book of Machabees, who ends his narrative by saying, "If I have done well, it is what I desired, but if not so perfectly, it must be pardoned me." What a contrast to St. Paul, who, speaking of his inspiration (1 Cor. vii, 40) and of his "weakness and fear" (*ibid.* ii, 4), does so in order to *boast* that his "speech was, not in the persuasive words of human wisdom, but in the showing of the Spirit and of power." The historian of the Machabees would have surely adopted a like tone of "glorying," had he had at the time a like consciousness of his divine gift.

§ 22.

Again, it follows from there being two agencies, divine grace and human intelligence, co-operating in the production of the Scriptures, that, whereas, if they were written, as in the Decalogue, by the immediate finger of God, every word of them must be His and His only; on the contrary, if they are man's writing, informed and quickened by the presence of the Holy Ghost, they admit, should it so happen, of being composed of outlying materials, which have passed through the minds and from the fingers of inspired penmen, and are known to be inspired on the ground that those who were the immediate editors, as they may be called, were inspired.

For an example of this we are supplied by the writer of the second book of Machabees, to which reference has already been made. "All such things," says the writer, "as have been comprised in five books by Jason of Cyrene, we have attempted to abridge in one book." Here we have the human aspect of an inspired work. Jason need not, the writer of the second book of Machabees must, have been inspired.

Again; St. Luke's Gospel is inspired, as having gone through and come forth from an inspired mind ; but the extrinsic sources of his narrative were not necessarily all inspired, any more than was Jason of Cyrene; yet such sources there were, for, in contrast with the testimony of the actual eye-witnesses of the events which he records, he says of himself that he wrote after a careful inquiry, "according as *they* delivered them to us, who from the beginning were eye-witnesses and ministers of the word;" as to himself, he had but "diligently attained to all things from the beginning." Here it was not the original statements, but his edition of them, which needed to be inspired.

§ 23.

Hence we have no reason to be surprised, nor is it against the faith to hold, that a canonical book may be composed, not only from, but even of, pre-existing documents, it being always borne in mind, as a necessary condition, that an inspired mind has exercised a supreme and an ultimate judgment on the work, determining what was to be selected and embodied in it, in order to its truth in all "matters of faith and morals pertaining to the edification of Christian doctrine," and its unadulterated truth.

Thus Moses may have incorporated in his manuscript as much from foreign documents as is commonly maintained by the critical school; yet the existing Pentateuch, with the miracles which it contains, may still (from that personal inspiration which belongs to a prophet) have flowed from his mind and hand on to his composition. He new-made and authenticated what till then was no matter of faith.

This being considered, it follows that a book may be, and may be accepted as, inspired, though not a word of it is an original document. Such is almost the case with the first book of Esdras. A learned writer in a publication of the day[1] says: "It consists of the contemporary historical journals, kept from time to time by the prophets or other authorised persons, who were eye-witnesses for the most part of what they record, and whose several narratives were afterwards strung together, and either abridged or added to, as the case required, by a later hand, of course an inspired hand."

And in like manner the Chaldee and Greek portions of the book of Daniel, even though not written by Daniel, may be, and we believe are, written by penmen inspired in matters of faith and morals; and so much, and nothing beyond, does the Church "oblige" us to believe.

§ 24.

I have said that the Chaldee, as well as the Hebrew portion of Daniel, requires, in order to its inspiration, not that it should be Daniel's writing, but that its writer, whoever he was, should be inspired. This leads me to the question whether inspiration requires and implies that the book inspired should, in its form and matter, be homogeneous, and all its parts belong to each other. Certainly not. The Book of Psalms is the obvious instance destructive of any such idea. What it really requires

---

[1] Smith's *Dictionary of the Bible*.

is an inspired Editor ;* that is, an inspired mind, authoritative in faith and morals, from whose fingers the sacred text passed. I believe it is allowed generally that, at the date of the captivity and under the persecution of Antiochus, the books of Scripture and the sacred text suffered much loss and injury. Originally the Psalms seem to have consisted of five books, of which only a portion, perhaps the first and second, were David's. That arrangement is now broken up, and the Council of Trent was so impressed with the difficulty of their authorship, that, in its formal decree respecting the Canon, instead of calling the collection "David's Psalms," as was usual, they called it the "Psalterium Davidicum," thereby meaning to imply, that, although canonical and inspired and in spiritual fellowship and relationship with those of "the choice Psalmist of Israel," the whole collection is not therefore necessarily the writing of David.

And as the name of David, though not really

---

* This representation must not be confused with either of the two views of canonicity which are pronounced insufficient by the Vatican Council, viz., 1, that in order to be sacred and canonical, it is enough for a book to be a work of mere human industry, provided it be afterwards approved by the authority of the Church ; and 2, that it is enough if it contains revealed teaching without error. Neither of these views supposes the presence of inspiration, whether in the writer or the writing ; what is contemplated above is an inspired writer in the exercise of his inspiration, and a work inspired from first to last under the action of that inspiration.

applicable to every Psalm, nevertheless protected and sanctioned them all, so the appendices which conclude the book of Daniel, Susanna and Bel, though not belonging to the main history, come under the shadow of that Divine Presence, which primarily rests on what goes before.

And so again, whether or not the last verses of St. Mark's, and two portions of St. John's Gospel, belong to those Evangelists respectively, matters not as regards their inspiration; for the Church has recognised them as portions of that sacred narrative which precedes or embraces them.

Nor does it matter, whether one or two Isaiahs wrote the book which bears that Prophet's name; the Church, without settling this point, pronounces it inspired in respect of faith and morals, both Isaiahs being inspired; and, if this be assured to us, all other questions are irrelevant and unnecessary.

Nor do the Councils forbid our holding that there are interpolations or additions in the sacred text, say, the last chapter of the Pentateuch, provided they are held to come from an inspired penman, such as Esdras, and are thereby authoritative in faith and morals.

§ 25.

From what has been last said it follows, that the titles of the Canonical books, and their ascription to definite authors, either do not come under their inspiration, or need not be accepted literally.

For instance: the Epistle to the Hebrews is said in our Bibles to be the writing of St. Paul, and so virtually it is, and to deny that it is so in any sense might be temerarious; but its authorship is not a matter of faith as its inspiration is, but an acceptance of received opinion, and because to no other writer can it be so well assigned.

Again, the 89th Psalm has for its title "A Prayer of Moses," yet that has not hindered a succession of Catholic writers, from Athanasius to Bellarmine, from denying it to be his.

Again, the Book of Wisdom professes (*e.g.*, chs. vii and ix) to be written by Solomon; yet our Bibles say, "It is written in the *person* of Solomon," and "it is uncertain who was the writer;" and St. Augustine, whose authority had so much influence in the settlement of the Canon, speaking of Wisdom and Ecclesiasticus, says: "The two books, by reason of a certain similarity of style, are usually called Solomon's, though the more learned have no doubt they do not belong to him." (Martin. *Pref. to Wisdom and Eccl.* ; Aug. *Opp.* t. iii, p. 733.)

If these instances hold, they are precedents for saying that it is no sin against the faith (for of such I have all along been speaking), nor indeed, if done conscientiously and on reasonable grounds, any sin, to hold that Ecclesiastes is not the writing of Solomon, in spite of its opening with a profession of being his; and that first, because that profession is a heading, not a portion of the book; secondly, because, even though it be part of the book, a like profession is made in the Book of Wisdom, without its being a proof that "Wisdom" is Solomon's; and thirdly, because such a profession may well be considered a prosopopœia not so difficult to understand as that of the Angel Raphael, when he called himself "the Son of the great Ananias."

On this subject Melchior Canus says: "It does not much matter to the Catholic Faith that a book was written by this or that writer, so long as the Spirit of God is believed to be the Author of it ; which Gregory delivers and explains in his Preface to Job, 'It matters not,' he says, 'with what pen the King has written His letter, if it be true that He has written it.'" (*Loc. Th.* p. 44.)

I say then of the Book of Ecclesiastes, its authorship is one of those questions which still lie in the hands of the Church. If the Church formally declared that it was written by Solomon, I consider that, in accordance with its heading (and, as implied in what follows, as in "Wisdom,") we should be bound, recollecting that she has the gift of judging "de vero sensu et interpretatione Scripturarum Sanctarum," to accept such a decree as a matter of faith; and in like manner, in spite of its heading, we should be bound to accept a contrary decree, if made to the effect that the book was not Solomon's. At present, as the Church (or Pope) has not pronounced on one side or on the other, I conceive that, till a decision comes from Rome, either opinion is open to the Catholic without any impeachment of his faith.

§ 26.

And here I am led on to inquire whether *obiter dicta* are conceivable in an inspired document. We know that they are held to exist, and even required, in treating of the dogmatic utterances of Popes, but are they compatible with inspiration? The common opinion is that they are not. Professor Lamy thus writes about them, in the form of an objection: "Many minute matters occur in the sacred writers which have regard only to human feebleness and the natural necessities of life, and by no means require inspiration, since they can otherwise be perfectly well known, and seem scarcely worthy of the Holy Spirit, as for instance what is said of the dog of Tobias, St. Paul's *penula*, and the salutations at the end of the Epistles." Neither he nor Fr. Patrizi allow of these exceptions; but Fr. Patrizi, as Lamy quotes him, "damnare non audet eos qui hæc tenerent," [viz., exceptions,] and he himself, by keeping silence, seems unable to condemn them either.

By *obiter dicta* in Scripture I also mean such statements as we find in the .Book of Judith, that Nabuchodonosor was King of Nineve. Now it is in favour of there being such unauthoritative *obiter dicta*, that, unlike those which occur in dogmatic utterances of Popes and Councils, they are, in Scripture, not doctrinal, but mere unimportant statements of fact ; whereas those of Popes and Councils may relate to faith and morals, and are said to be uttered *obiter*, because they are not contained within the scope of the formal definition, and imply no intention of binding the consciences of the faithful. There does not then seem any serious difficulty in admitting their existence in Scripture. Let it be observed, its miracles are doctrinal facts, and in no sense of the phrase can be considered *obiter dicta.*

§ 27.

It may be questioned, too, whether the absence of chronological sequence might not be represented as an infringement of plenary inspiration more serious than the *obiter dicta* of which I have been speaking. Yet St. Matthew is admitted by approved commentators to be unsolicitous as to order of time. So says Fr. Patrizi (*De Evang.* lib. ii, p. 1), viz., "Matthæum de observando temporis ordine minime sollicitum esse." He gives instances, and then repeats " Matthew did not observe order of time." If such absence of order is compatible with inspiration in St. Matthew, as it is, it might be consistent with inspiration in parts of the Old Testament, supposing they are open to re-arrangement in chronology. Does not this teach us to fall back upon the decision of the Councils that "faith and morals pertaining to the edification of Christian doctrine" are the scope, the true scope, of inspiration? And is not the Holy See the judge given us for determining what is for edification and what is not?

There is another practical exception to the ideal continuity of Scripture inspiration in mere matters of fact, and that is the multitude of various manuscript readings which surround the sacred text. Unless we have the text as inspired men wrote it, we have not the divine gift in its fulness, and as far as we have no certainty which out of many is the true reading, so far, wherever the sense is affected, we are in the same difficulty as may be the consequence of an *obiter dictum*. Yet, in spite of this danger, even cautious theologians do not hesitate to apply the gratuitous hypothesis of errors in transcription as a means of accounting for such statements of fact as they feel to need an explanation. Thus Fr. Patrizi, not favouring the order of our Lord's three temptations in the desert, as given by St. Luke, attributes it to the mistake of the transcribers. "I have no doubt at all," he says, "that it is to be attributed, not to Luke himself, but to his transcribers" (*ibid.* p. 5) ; and again, he says that it is owing "vitio librariorum" (p. 394). If I recollect rightly, Melchior Canus has recourse to the "fault of transcribers" also. Indeed it is commonly urged in controversy (*vide* Lamy, i. p. 31).

§ 28.

I do not here go on to treat of the special instance urged against us by M. Renan, drawn from the Book of Judith, because I have wished to lay down principles, and next, because his charge can neither be proved nor refuted just now, while the strange discoveries are in progress about Assyrian and Persian history by means of the cuneiform inscriptions. When the need comes, the Church, or the Holy See, will interpret the sacred book for us.

I conclude by reminding the reader that in these remarks I have been concerned only with the question—what have Catholics to hold and profess *de fide* about Scripture? that is, what it is the Church "insists" on their holding; and next, by unreservedly submitting what I have written to the judgment of the Holy See, being more desirous that the question should be satisfactorily answered, than that my own answer should prove to be in every respect the right one.

JOHN H. CARDINAL NEWMAN.

§ 29.

NOTE.

On the Phrase "Auctor utriusque Testamenti" in the Councils.

Does it mean Inspirer of the Scriptures, or Author of the two Dispensations or Covenants—viz., of the Old as well as of the New?

I consider it has the latter meaning, being directed against the heresy, so early and so late, of Gnostics, Manichees, Priscillianists, and Paulicians, that the God of the Old Testament was not the God of the New. On the contrary, in a succession of protests, the Church from the beginning asserts that there is but one God of both Dispensations; that one and the same God is the Author of the one and the other. He who originated the New Covenant also originated the Old. The heresy anathematised was not that the Scriptures were not inspired, but that the God of the New Dispensation was not the God of the Old.

1. St. Irenæus, A.D. 200, is one of the earliest writers who protests against this heretical doctrine, and he throws light upon a subsequent series of Councils down to the Tridentine. He never confuses between "Testaments" and "Scriptures;" with him, Testament means Covenant or Dispensation. Sometimes he speaks of the Old Testament as "The Law," as our Lord speaks of "The Law and the Prophets," not Prophetic writings.

D

The New Testament he calls the Gospel—viz., in the abstract. In one place he speaks of *four* Testaments, those of Adam, Noe, Moses, and Christ. *Contra Hæreses*, Liber iii, c. xi, § 8. Speaking of the two, he says, "Non alterum [Auctorem] Vetera, alterum proferentem Nova docuit, sed *unum et eundem*." Liber iv, c. ix, § 1. Again, "*Utraque* Testamenta *unus et idem* Paterfamilias produxit." *Ibid*.

2. So the Spanish and Portuguese Council of A.D. 447 against the Priscillianists, "Si quis dixerit *alterum* Deum esse priscæ Legis, *alterum* Evangeliorum, anathema sit."

3. Again, "Credo Novi et Veteris Testamenti, Legis, et Prophetarum et Apostolorum, *unum* esse Auctorem, Deum Omnipotentem," &c. S. Leo IX, A.D. 1050.

4. The profession of the Waldenses on their submission, "Novi et Veteris Testamenti *unum eundem* Auctorem esse Dominum credimus." A.D. 1210.

5. "Credimus Novi et Veteris Testamenti, Legis ac Prophetarum et Apostolorum, *unum* esse Auctorem Deum." *Conf. M. Palæolog.*, A.D. 1274.

6. Pope Eugenius IV, A.D. 1439. "*Unum atque eundem* Deum Veteris et Novi Testamenti, hoc est, Legis et Prophetarum, atque Evangelii, profitetur Auctorem, quoniam, eodem Spiritu Sancto inspirante, *utriusque* Testamenti *Sancti* locuti sunt, quorum *libros* suscipit et veneratur."

7. Council of Trent. It only goes as far as

Irenæus. "Omnes *libros* tam Veteris quam Novi Testamenti, cum *utriusque* [not omnium] *unus* Deus sit auctor, ... *suscipit* et veneratur."

8. It is true that the Vatican Council has made the words "Auctor Scripturarum" equivalent to "Inspiration," but when it so spoke it was engaged upon the subject of "morals and religion," not upon profane history, &c. *Vide* Abp. Mac Evilly; 2 Timothy, c. iii, v. 16, 17. *

---

* "In the Greek, the word 'is' is understood, so as to convey two assertions : first, all Scripture is inspired of God ; and secondly, Scripture thus inspired is also useful for the purposes of instruction, &c. According to our Vulgate reading there is only one assertion conveyed, viz., that all Scripture that is inspired of God is profitable for instructing the ignorant in the truths of faith, for refuting the errors opposed to sound doctrine, for rebuking men of corrupt principles and morals, and for forming men to sanctity and Christian justice. These are the four great duties of a minister of religion, and for these the S. Scripture is profitable. It is quite evident that this passage furnishes no argument whatever that the S. Scripture, without Tradition, is the *sole* *rule of faith;* for, although S. Scripture is *profitable* for these four ends, still it is not said to be *sufficient.* The Apostle requires the aid of Tradition (2 Thessalonians, ii, 15). Moreover, the Apostle here refers to the Scriptures which Timothy was taught in his infancy. Now, a good part of the New Testament was not written in his boyhood : some of the Catholic Epistles were not written even when St. Paul wrote this, and none of the Books of the New Testament were then placed on the canon of the Scripture books. He refers, then, to the Scriptures of the *Old* Testament, and if the argument from this passage proved anything, it would prove too much, viz., that the Scriptures of the *New* Testament were not necessary for a rule of faith.

It is hardly necessary to remark that this passage furnishes no proof of the inspiration of the several books of S. Scripture, even of those admitted to be such. According to the Vulgate reading of this verse (16), which Bloomfield assures us is adopted by all the most eminent critics after Theodoret, there is nothing said of the inspiration of any part of Scripture ; all that is stated is simply this : that every portion of inspired Scripture is profitable for teaching, reproving, &c., without determining what these inspired Scriptures are. Nor is the question determined by the Greek reading either. For we are not told what is meant by 'every Scripture' of which it is said, according to this reading, that it 'is inspired,' or what the Books or portions of 'inspired Scripture' are."

ESSAY II.

ESSAY II.

§ 30.

Prefatory Notice.

IN the February Number of the *Nineteenth Century,* an article of mine appeared, which has elicited a criticism from a Catholic Professor of name. As I acquiesce neither in his statements nor in his reasonings, I have been led to put on paper Remarks in answer to him ; and that without availing myself of the offer made to me by the Editor of the Review to re-publish, together with these Remarks, my Article itself : an indulgence beyond its rules, which I feel I have no right to accept, unless the Article shall be expressly called for by the public.

At present, in order to make these Remarks intelligible to those who have not seen my original Article, it is sufficient, I conceive, to say that they aim, as that Article did, at answering the question proposed in my title-page*: " What is of obligation

---

* The original title-page.

for a Catholic to believe concerning the Inspiration of the Canonical Scriptures?" This being the sole question, I observed, that, since two Ecumenical Councils have spoken upon Inspiration, it is obvious to have recourse to them, if we would learn what is *de fide*, or obligatory on our faith in the matter. To this, of course, must be added any teaching which comes to us incidentally from the ordinary *magisterium* of the Church, or from the joint testimony of the Fathers; but the two Councils, the Tridentine and the Vatican, give us by far the most distinct and definite information.

These two Councils decide that the Scriptures are inspired, and inspired throughout, but they do not add to their decision that they are inspired by an immediately divine act, but they say that they are inspired through the instrumentality of inspired men; that they are inspired in all matters of faith and morals, meaning thereby, not only theological doctrine, but also the historical and prophetical narratives which they contain, from Genesis to the Acts of the Apostles; and lastly, that, being inspired because written by inspired men, they have a human side, which manifests itself in language, style, tone of thought, character, intellectual peculiarities, and such infirmities, not sinful, as belong to our nature, and which in unimportant matters may issue in what in doctrinal definitions is called an *obiter dictum*. At the same time, the gift of inspiration being divine, a Catholic must never forget that what he is handling is in a true sense the Word of God, which, as I said in my Article, "by reason of the difficulty of always drawing the line between what is human and what is divine, cannot be put on the level of other books, as it is now the fashion to do, but has the nature of a Sacrament, which is outward and inward, and a channel of supernatural grace."

This is why the second great definition of the Councils, on which I proceeded in my Article to insist, is so important, viz., that "the authoritative interpretation of Scripture rests with the Church."

So much on the view of Scripture which offends the Professor in question, to whose criticisms in the March Number of the *Irish Ecclesiastical Record* I now make my answer.

§ 31.

Prefatory Notice (continued).

A not over-courteous, nor over-exact writer, in his criticisms on my Essay on Inspiration, gives it as his judgment upon it, that "its startling character" must be evident to "the merest tyro in the schools of Catholic Theology." 'Tis a pity he did not take more than a short month for reading, pondering, writing, and printing. Had he not been in a hurry to publish, he would have made a better Article. I took above a twelve-month for mine. Thus I account for some of the Professor's unnecessary remarks.

If I understand him, his main *thesis* is this— that, virtually or actually, Scripture is inspired, not only in matters of faith and morals, as is declared in the Councils of Trent and of the Vatican, but in all respects, and for all purposes, and on all subjects ; so that no clause all through the Bible is liable to criticism of any kind, and that no good Catholic can think otherwise. If this is his position, it is plain that I approach the question on quite a distinct side from his ; but I do not see that personally and practically I have very much to differ from him in, except in his faulty logic, and his misrepresentations of what I have written.

§ 32.

Divine Inspiration of Scripture in all matters of Faith and Morals.

This proposition must be accepted as *de fide*, or of obligatory faith, by every Catholic, as having been so defined by the Councils of Trent and of the Vatican.

Now I say first, that the inspiration of religious and moral truth, of which these Councils speak, is a divine gift, in the first instance given to divine ministers, and from them carried on, as into their oral teachings, so also into such of their writings as the Church has declared to be sacred and canonical.

And next: divine gifts, as we read of them in the history of Revelation, did not extend in every case to all departments of ministration, but had in each instance a particular service and application. These various favours were ordinarily but partial, given for precise and definite purposes; so that it is but in harmony with the rule of Providence in parallel cases, if there should be found, in respect to Biblical Inspiration, a distribution and a limitation in the bestowal of it. St. Paul's account of the *gratiæ gratis datæ*, may be taken to illustrate this principle, without my meaning at all thereby to imply that the inspiration of an Evangelist was not in its intensity, refinement, abundance, and manifoldness, far superior to the gifts spoken of by the Apostle in the chapter to which I refer. I refer to that chapter in order to draw attention to what was the rule of Providence at the first in the disposal and direction of the *gratiæ gratis datæ*, viz., that they had a special scope and character, and, in consequence, as is intimated in the parable of the Five and Ten Talents, were limited in their range of operation. I am not here affirming or denying that Scripture is inspired in matters of astronomy and chronology, as well as in faith and morals; but I certainly do not see that because Inspiration is given for the latter subjects, therefore it extends to the former.

The Apostle tells us that, whereas there are "*diversities* of grace," there is "the *same* Spirit"; and that "the manifestation of the Spirit is given to every man *unto profit*"; that is, the gift is given according to the measure of the need. Then he says, "To one by the Spirit is given the Word of Wisdom, to another the Word of Knowledge according to the same Spirit." To both of them there was given "the Word" of God; but one was the minister of the Word as far as Wisdom went, and the other as far as Knowledge went; and, though the same man might indeed have both gifts, we could not logically argue that he had wisdom on the mere ground of his having knowledge.

It may be observed too that it was by information from those who thus had "the Word" of God that St. Luke wrote his Gospel; for he says expressly that the things which he recorded "were delivered to us" by those "who from the beginning were eye-witnesses, and servants of the *Word*"; that is, those who saw, or who were inspired to know, what the Evangelist reported from them: a statement which would imply that their particular gift was that of bearing faithful witness, or otherwise being endowed with the gift of knowledge. As another instance of the limitation of a gift, I may refer to the history of Jonas. "The Word of the Lord" came to him to denounce judgment against Nineve; but he did not know that the divine menace was conditional. Again, Eliseus says to Giezi, "Was not my *heart present* when the man turned back to meet thee ? " yet, when the Sunamitess had "caught hold on his feet," he had said, "Her soul is in anguish, and the Lord hath hid it from me and hath not told me."

I return to St. Paul : he continues, "To another, Faith in the same Spirit ; to another, the grace of healing in one Spirit; to another, the working of miracles ; to another, prophecy," and so on. He ends a long chapter on the subject by enumerating the offices which needed and determined the gifts— "Apostles, Prophets, Doctors," and the rest ; and by intimating that, as not all are Apostles or Prophets, so the gifts, necessary to these, were not given to others. This is from 1 Cor. xii. The 4th Chapter of his epistle to the Ephesians is on the same subject.

I should infer from this, that those who were chosen by the Spirit to minister between God and man, such as Moses, Samuel, Elias, Isaias, the Apostles and Evangelists, would be invested with the high gifts necessary for their work, and not necessarily with other gifts.

I do not, then, feel it any difficulty when I am told by the infallible voice of more than one Ecumenical Council, that the writers of Scripture, whether under the New Covenant or the Old, ethical and religious writers as they were, have had assigned to them a gift and promise in teaching which is in keeping with this antecedent idea which we form of the work of Evangelists and Prophets. If they are to teach us our duty to God and man, it is natural that inspiration should be promised them in matters of faith and morals; and if such is the actual promise, it is natural that Councils should insist upon its being such;—but how otherwise are we to account for the remarkable stress laid on the inspiration of Scripture in matters of faith and morals, both in the Vatican and at Trent, if after all faith and morals, in view of inspiration, are only parts of a larger gift? Why was it not simply said once for all that in all matters of faith or fact, not only in all its parts, but on every subject whatever, Scripture was inspired? If nothing short of the highest and exactest truth on all subjects must be contemplated as the gift conveyed to the inspired writers, what is gained by singling out faith and morals as the legitimate province of Inspiration, and thereby throwing the wider and more complete view of Scripture truth into the shade? Why, on the contrary, does the Vatican Council so carefully repeat the very wording of the Tridentine in its statements about inspiration in faith and morals, putting no other subject matter on a level with them? It may perhaps be said that it is a rule with Councils, that the later repeat the very words of the earlier ; true, the Holy Trinity, the Creation, the Incarnation, the Blessed Virgin's prerogatives, are often expressed in language carrying on a tradition of terms as well as truths ; but this is done because the truths or words are important. It is a paradox to say that the Vatican declarations about Scripture are in their wording so much of a *fac simile* of the Tridentine, only because they mean so very little. Even when a phrase is not easy to translate, the identity is preserved ; for instance, the clause "in rebus fidei et morum, ad ædificationem doctrinæ Christianæ pertinentium," not "pertinentibus," is found in both Councils.

This is the obvious aspect under which I first view the inspiration of Scripture, as determined by the Councils.

§ 33.

Inspiration in matters of Historical Fact.

Here we are brought to a second and most important question. When I say that the writers of Scripture were divinely inspired in all matters of faith and morals, what matters are included in the range of such inspiration ? Are historical statements of fact included ? It makes me smile to think that any one could fancy me so absurd as to exclude them, especially since in a long passage in my Essay I have expressly included them ; but the Professor has done his best so to manage my text, as to make his readers believe that the Bible, as far as it is historical, does not in my view proceed from inspired writers. Professing to quote me, he omits just the very passage in which I have distinctly avowed the inspiration of the whole of its history. This is so strange, so anomalous a proceeding, as to make it difficult to believe that the same person who had the good feeling to write the first page of the Review wrote those which follow.

I am obliged to take notice of this great impropriety in pure self-defence; for if I am not able to show that the writer has ill-treated me, he will have an argument against me stronger than any which by fair means he is able to produce. On the other hand, if I show that he has been guilty of an indefensible act, third parties will not be so ready to think him a safe guide in other judgments which he makes to my discredit.

To begin, then: in § 13 of my Essay, pp. 5, 6, I write thus: "While the Councils, as has been shown, lay down so emphatically the inspiration of Scripture in respect to faith and morals, it is remarkable that they do not say a word directly as to its inspiration in matters of fact. Yet are we therefore to conclude that the record of facts in Scripture does not come under the guarantee of its inspiration? *we are not so to conclude.*"

These are my words, as they stand; but he quotes them thus: "[The Cardinal] asserts that, while the Councils, as has been shown, lay down so emphatically the inspiration of Scripture in respect to faith and morals, it is remarkable that they do not say a word directly as to its inspiration in matters of fact," p. 139; *and there he stops:* he quotes neither my question nor my answer which follow, my question being,

Qu.: "Are we therefore to conclude that the record of facts in Scripture does not come under the guarantee of its inspiration ? "

and my answer being,

Answ.: "We are not so to conclude, and for this plain reason," &c., &c.

With such notions of a critic's duty, much less does the Professor think it necessary to quote, or, I suppose, even to read, the twenty lines on behalf of the inspiration of the Bible history which follow thus:

"For this plain reason—the sacred narrative, carried on through so many ages, what is it but the very matter for our faith and rule of our obedience ? What but that narrative itself is the supernatural teaching, in order to which inspiration is given ? What is the whole history, traced out in Scripture from Genesis to Esdras, and thence on to the end of the Acts of the Apostles, but a manifestation of Divine Providence, on the one hand interpretative, on a large scale and with analogical applications, of universal history, and on the other preparatory, typical and predictive, of the Evangelical Dispensation ? Its pages breathe of providence and grace, of our Lord, and of His work and teaching, from beginning to end. It views facts in those relations in which neither ancients, such as the Greek and Latin classical historians, nor moderns, such as

E

Niebuhr, Grote, Ewald, or Michelet, can view them. In this point of view it has God for its Author, even though the finger of God traced no words but the Decalogue. Such is the claim of Bible history in its substantial fulness to be accepted *de fide* as true. *In this point of view, Scripture is inspired, not only in faith and morals, but in all its parts which bear on faith, including matters of fact.*"

All this he leaves out.

If a finish was wanting to this specimen of, what I must call, sharp practice, he has taken care to supply it. For, after cutting off my own statement at its third line, as I have shown, he substitutes, as if mine, a statement of his own, which he attributes to me, about *obiter dicta*, adding the words, "*Hence* he [the Cardinal] raises the question," which I do not raise till eight pages later, and not "hence" even then. And next, whereas *obiter dicta* are according to him in their very nature exceptions to a rule, viz., the rule that Scripture statements of fact are inspired, he is obliged for the moment to imply that I do maintain the rule, in order that he may be able to impute to me, in cases of *obiter dicta*, a breach of it.

§ 34.

Obiter Dicta viewed relatively to Inspiration.

The subject which naturally comes next to be considered is that of the possible presence of *obiter dicta* in inspired Scripture; by *obiter dicta* being meant phrases, clauses, or sentences in Scripture about matters of mere fact, which, as not relating to faith and morals, may without violence be referred to the human element in its composition.

Here, however, I observe with satisfaction that the Professor so far does me justice as to allow that what I have conceded, or have proposed to concede, to the scientific or literary inquirer, is not inconsistent with what the Church pronounces to be obligatory *de fide* on the Catholic. He says, "while the Church is silent, we of course do not dare to censure these views, but neither do we dare to hold them." This being the case, I shall, in the interest of the untheological student, under correction of the Church, continue as I have begun, to treat my subject as a question open to argument.

1. Now I observe, first, that any statement about the inspiration of Scripture is far too serious a matter in its bearings to be treated carelessly; and consequently the Professor explains, while he complains of, my "raising the question" of *obiter dicta* "and not answering it." Of course; I do not go further in my Essay than saying, "There does not seem any serious difficulty in admitting" that they are to be found in Scripture. Why is not that enough for a cautious man to say? The decision of the point does not rest with me; but still I may have an opinion as long as there is no decision.

2. And next, why does he always associate an *obiter dictum* with the notion of error or moral infirmity, or, even as he sometimes expresses himself, with *"falsehood"*? At least what right has he to attribute such an association to me? I have implied no such thing. I very much doubt whether I have even once used the word "error" in connection with the phrase "obiter dictum," though (as I shall show directly) no harm follows if I have. I have given my own sense of the word when I parallel it to such instances of it as occur in a question of dogma. Does the Professor mean to say that such a *dictum* is necessarily false when it occurs in a dogmatic document? No—it is merely unauthoritative. Mind, I am not arguing that such an unauthoritative *dictum* is possible in a matter of inspired Scripture on the ground that it is possible in a matter of dogma; but I am showing by a parallel case what my own meaning of the word is.

Obiter dictum means, as I understand it, a phrase or sentence which, whether a statement of literal fact or not, is not from the circumstances binding on our faith. The force of the *"obiter"* is negative, not positive. To say, "I do not accept a statement as a literal fact," is not all one with saying that it is *not* a fact; I can *not hold* without *holding not*. The very comfort of an *obiter dictum* to the Catholic, whether in its relation to infallibility or to inspiration, whether in dogma or in Scripture, is, that it enables him in controversy to pass by a difficulty, which else may be pressed on him without his having the learning perhaps, or the knowledge, or the talent, to answer it; that it enables him to profess neither Yes nor No in questions which are beyond him, and on which nothing depends. In difficult questions it leaves the Catholic student in peace. And, if my Critic asks, as I understand him to do, who shall decide what is important and what is not, I answer at once, the Church, which, though he seems to forget it, claims the supreme interpretation of Scripture according to the force of that second dogma about the written Word which was defined both at Trent and the Vatican.

It is plain then, as an *obiter dictum*, in my understanding of it, does not oblige us to affirm or to deny the literal sense, neither does it prohibit us from passing over the literal sense altogether, and, if we prefer, from taking some second, third, or fourth interpretation of the many which are possible, (provided the Church does not forbid,) as I shall show from St. Thomas presently.

3. And now take one of the instances with which Scripture may be said to provide us. St. Paul speaks of "the cloak which he left at Troas with Carpus." Would St. Timothy, to whom he wrote, think this an infallible utterance? And supposing it had been discovered, on most plausible evidence, that the Apostle left his cloak with Eutychus, not with Carpus, would Timothy, would Catholics now, make themselves unhappy, because St. Paul had committed

what the Professor calls "a falsehood"? Would Christians declare that they had no longer any confidence in Paul after he had so clearly shown that he "had" *not* "the Spirit of God"? Would they feel that he had put the whole Apostolic system into confusion, and by mistaking Eutychus for Carpus he had deprived them henceforth of reading with any comfort his Epistle to the Romans or to the Ephesians?

I fear seeming to use light words on a sacred subject; but I must ask, is St. Paul's request to Timothy about his *penula*, a portion of "the Word"? is it more than an apparent exception, in the text of his Epistle, to the continuity of the Divine Inspiration? And was not that continuity still without any break at all in St. Paul, if we consider Inspiration as a supernatural habit? May I ask an urgent, important question without profaneness? Could St. Paul say, "Thus saith the Lord, Send the penula," &c., &c.? I do not deny, however, that in a certain case he could so speak; but are we driven to that hypothesis here?

Theology has its prerogatives and rights; but its very perfection as a science causes theologians to be somewhat wanting in tenderness to concrete humanity, to those lay Catholics who in their grasp of religious truth do not go much beyond the catechism, and who, without entering into the expedients which system demands, wish to preserve their obedience to Holy Church.

4. Let us see, however, whether St. Thomas, the greatest of theologians, will not accompany at least my first step in this question.

In his Summa, i, qu. 102, he takes for granted the Inspiration of Scripture, and its truthfulness as the consequence of that inspiration; for where truth is not an effect, inspiration is not a cause. And he inquires what statements of fact in Scripture are to be taken as true literally, and what are not; and, in answer to the question, he lays down, as a rule or test, decisive of the point, this circumstance, viz., whether the *manner* or *bearing* of the sacred writer is historical or not. This being kept in mind, let us consider his words:—

"In omnibus quæ *sic* [per modum narrationis historicæ] Scriptura tradit, est pro fundamento tenenda veritas historiæ"; that is, "In all matters which Scripture delivers after the manner of historical narrative, we must hold, as a fundamental fact, the truth of the history."

Now observe what follows from this. In giving a *rule* or *test* of the *truth* of historical statements, he surely implies that there are, or at least that there may be, statements which do *not* embody, which do not profess to embody, historical truth. If, in a military gathering or review, I were told, "You may know the English by their red coats," would not this imply that there were troops on the ground who were *not* English and *not* in red? And in like manner, when St. Thomas says that the test of historical truth is the inspired penman's writing in the historical style, he certainly implies that there are, or might be, statements of fact, which in their literal sense come short of the historic style and of historic truth, or are what I should call *obiter dicta*. I repeat, *obiter dicta* are but "unhistoric statements." So far I consider I speak with the sanction of St. Thomas; now let me go on to say what I hold without (as I fear) his sanction.

5. I feel very diffident of my ability to speak with ever so much restraint of the words of St. Thomas; but, if I am forced to speak, certainly he seems to me not only to hold as literal truth that " Paradisus est locus corporeus," which is the matter before him, but to see little difficulty, supposing (which of course he does not grant) that the literal sense was not historic, or was doubtful, in interpreting the whole account spiritually or even figuratively. Therefore, if the case occurred of small inaccuracies of fact in Scripture history, instead of countenancing me in saying that, in matters which did not infringe upon faith and morals, such apparent error was of no serious consequence, I grant that he would have preferred, (and with St. Augustine,) to interpret a passage, so characterised, in a spiritual sense, or according to some other secondary sense, which he thinks it possible to give to Scripture. Here it is, I grant, that I should not have his countenance; he would not indeed forbid me to say that a statement was *literally* inaccurate, but he would rather wish me to find some

interpretation for it which would give it an edifying sense. Thus St. Augustine, when questioned as to Jacob's conduct towards his father and brother, appeals from that grave question to its typical and evangelical meaning: "Non est mendacium, sed mysterium." What makes me so conclude is a passage in his Quæst. iii de Potentia. He there speaks of the danger, "ne aliquis ita Scripturam ad unum sensum cogere velit, quod alios sensus, qui in se veritatem continent, et possunt, salvâ circumstantia litteræ, Scripturæ aptari, penitus excludantur." Then he says that the dignity of Scripture requires many senses under one letter. He concludes by saying, "Omnis veritas, quæ, salvâ litteræ circumstantia, potest divinæ Scripturæ aptari, *est ejus sensus.*"

§ 35.

Restrictions upon Inspiration.

St. Augustine and St. Thomas are such great names in the Church that he must be a bold Catholic, who, knowing what they are, should contradict them. But they cannot rightly be taken instead of *her* Voice. There are numbers of good Catholics who never heard of them, and many of these learned and accomplished in their respective ways and callings, and earnestly desirous to remain in the faith and fear of Holy Church. And, as I would not dare to treat the above-mentioned

Fathers with disrespect, much less should I dare to
speak against the teaching of the Church herself;
and when the Church has distinctly taught us in
two Ecumenical Councils, once and again, at the
interval of three hundred years, and in very different
conditions of human society, that the divine inspiration of Scripture is to be assigned especially *rebus
fidei et morum*, it shocks me to find a Catholic
Professor asserting that such a dogmatic decision is
what he calls a *restriction;* a charge as inconsistent
with good logic as with tenderness towards a decision
of the Church. Of course I have no intention of
complaining of his adding to the Church's decision
the conclusions of theology or the anticipations of
devotion, but her person (if I may so speak of the
Church) is sacred; and she has reasons for all she
does, and all she does not do. We should never
forget who is minister and who is Lord.

So much for (what I fear I must call) the
impropriety of the word "restriction" when applied
to a literal quotation of mine from the definitions
of two Ecumenical Councils. Now for its failure
in logic.

The Professor affirms, speaking (as I understand
him) of what he seems to consider in this case not
more than an hypothesis, namely, the "clause" *in
rebus fidei et morum*, that it is "a restricting clause,"
and that "the Catholic dogma is adequately and
accurately expressed only by *eliminating* that clause."
Eliminating! He cannot be using so great a word

with reference to any mere statement of mine; it fits on to nothing short of the dogmatic utterances of the two Ecumenical Councils. He has said nothing in order to guard against this natural conclusion, and as if to make it the clearer, he contrasts it with my own words, to the effect that " sacred Scripture is inspired *throughout.*"

But I would observe, that, easy as it is to speak against " restrictions " being placed on the gift of inspiration, those who would impute the blame, whether to the Church or to me, are also incurring it themselves. For instance, if Scripture is the Word of God (as in a true sense it is), and inspiration is (in the Professor's sense) *throughout* it, it cannot but be *verbally* inspired; but the prevalent opinion now is that this is not the case. How is this not putting a restriction upon inspiration? How. is it *thorough*, if the *language* of Scripture is not included in it? Yet the Professor, who is so disturbed at my appealing to the dogmatic force of "*fides et mores,*" has no scruple whatever in depriving inspiration of its action upon the language of the writers of Scripture. He ventures to say, in spite of the dissent of great Fathers, that " God in most cases *did* leave the choice of the words to the writer"; and he speaks of the opinion, that the Holy Spirit dictated the sacred books word for word, as having been "held by a few, and now generally and justly rejected." Thus he speaks. It seems that he may say *without* Ecumenical Councils what another may not say *with* them.

Nor is this the only "restriction" which he allows upon the inspiration of Scripture. He does not quite commit himself to it as an opinion, but he does not quarrel with those who hold it, viz., that inspiration goes as far as, but not further than, the "*res et sententias*" of Scripture, beyond which, it seems, the inspiration does not reach; he calls for no "eliminating" process here.

But something more has to be said still on the Professor's mode of arguing. Nothing is more difficult in controversy than the skilful use of metaphors. A metaphor has a dozen aspects, and, unless we look sharp, we shall be slain by the rebound of one or other of our deductions from them. Now if there be an idea intimately connected or present to us when in theology we speak of a "*word*," it is that of a personal agent, from whom the word proceeds. It is an effect which does not exist without a cause. It must have a speaker or writer, and but one such. In this case one effect cannot have two causes. If two are ascribed to it, one or other must be ascribed metaphorically. We cannot refer it to each of two causes at one time in its full sense. But the Professor takes it in its highest sense, as the Word of God, when he would prove that Scripture had no imperfection in it; yet when he would relieve himself of the difficulties, and account for defects, of language, then it is the word of man. Of course the inspiration of Scripture is from above; but what I want to be told is, are we to consider a book of Scripture, whether written or spoken, literally the Word of God or literally the word of man?

§ 36.

Plenary as well as Present Inspiration.

But it may be objected, in answer to what I have been saying in explanation of "restriction," that the Council of the Vatican, treating of inspiration, has added to the dogma of Trent a clause which destroys the distinction which I have been making as to the special object with reference to which the sacred writers were endowed with the gift. For the Vatican Council has dogmatically determined the books of holy Scripture, "libros *integros cum omnibus suis partibus,* inspiratos esse"; and if the whole of Scripture in all its parts is inspired, how can inspiration be restricted to the matters of faith and morals? Yet I conceive this difficulty admits of an easy reply.

Certainly I have no wish to explain away the words of the Council; but is there no distinction between a gift itself, and the purpose for which it was made, and the use to which it is to be applied? We meet with this distinction every day. Might not a benefactor leave a legacy to the whole of a large family of children, one and all, yet under the condition that it was expended solely on their education ? And so Scripture is inspired in its length and breadth, and is brought into the compass of one volume by virtue of this supernatural bond; whenever, wherever, and by whomsoever written, it is all inspired : still we may ask the question, In what respect, and for what purpose ?

When we speak of the Bible in its length and breadth, we speak of it quantitatively ; but this does not interfere with our viewing it in relation to the character, or what may be called the quality, of the inspiration. According to the two Councils, Scripture is inspired as being the work of inspired men, the subject of faith and morals being the occupation or mission assigned to them and their writings, and inspiration being the efficient cause of their teaching.

Each of these truths is independent of, is consistent with, each. The plenary extent of inspiration, and the definite object of it, neither of these can interfere, neither can be confused, with the other. Because a cup is full, that does not enable us to determine what is the nature and the effects of the liquor with which it is filled; whether, for instance, it is nutritive or medicinal or merely restorative ; and so, though Scripture be plenarily inspired, it is a question still, for what purposes, and in what way.

In a word, Inspiration of Scripture in omnibus *suis partibus* is one thing; in omnibus *rebus* is another.

It may be asked how inspiration could be given

to the Sacred Writers for faith and morals, whereas they were not always writing, and when they did write, needed not be writing on religious and ethical subjects. Thus St. Paul, when he wrote about his *penula*, was he not in possession of a divine gift which on that occasion he could not use? But we see instances of this every day. A man may be strong without opportunity of using his strength, and a man may have a good memory or be a good linguist though he exercises his gift only now and then; and so a passage of Scripture may have spiritual meanings, as St. Thomas would hold, and may avail for edification with a force which an uninspired writing has not, though the literal sense may refer to matters purely secular and human, as the passage in John ii, 10, which I have quoted in my Article.

§ 37.

Inspiration as Co-ordinate with Error.

There is one subject more, on which it may be expedient to dwell for a few minutes.

The Professor insists on its being a conclusion theologically certain that everything that is to be found in the Sacred Writers is literally the Word of God; and in consequence he would imply that I, by questioning whether some words in Scripture may not come from the writers themselves mainly, have committed the serious act of rejecting a theological truth. Now, of course it is indisputable that a proposition, which is the immediate consequence of a truth of Revelation, is itself a certain truth. Certainly; but it is a further question whether this or that conclusion is an instance of such a real demonstration. This indeed I say frankly, that, if my certainties depended on the Professor's syllogisms, I should have small chance of making a decent show of theological certainties.

For instance, in the present question, he has proved just the contrary to what he meant to prove, as can easily be shown. He had to prove that it is theologically certain that the whole of Scripture, whatever is contained in it, is the Word of God, and this is how he does it. He says, "It is as absurd to say that a man could commit sin under the *impulse* of the Holy Ghost, as to say that the Sacred Writers could write error under the inspiration of the Holy Ghost." Why does he change "impulse" into "inspiration" in the second clause of his sentence? Who ever fancied that the *impulse* of the Holy Spirit might cause error? Who will deny that the impulse of the Holy Spirit would certainly be accorded to an Apostle or Prophet to hinder, even in a statement of fact, any serious error? If the Holy Spirit does not hinder varieties and errors in transcribers of Scripture which damage the perfection of His work, why should He hinder small errors (on the hypothesis that such there are)

of the original writers ? Is not He, with the Church
co-operating, sufficient for a Guardian ?

But this is not all. He says that error cannot
co-exist with inspiration, more than sin with grace;
but grace *can* co-exist with sin. His parallel just
turns against him. Good Christians are each " the
Temple of God," "partakers of the Divine Nature,"
nay " gods," and they are said " portare Deum in
corpore suo "; and priests, I consider, have not less
holiness than others; yet every priest in his daily
Mass asks pardon "pro innumerabilibus peccatis et
offensionibus et negligentiis meis." Grace brings a
soul nearer to God than inspiration, for Balaam and
Caiphas were inspired; yet the Professor tells us
that, though sin is possible in spite of grace, error
is impossible because of inspiration.

Thus I answer the special remarks made by my
Critic on my February Article; should other objections be urged against it, I trust they would be
found to admit of as direct an explanation.

J. H. N.

May, 1884.

ESSAY III.

ESSAY III.

REVELATION IN ITS RELATION TO FAITH.

§ 38.

The Author's view of "Reason."

It would be easy to expose the errors about me, both in fact and in logic, for which Principal Fairbairn has made himself responsible in his May article in *The Contemporary Review*, but that would not answer the purpose which leads me to write. Such an outlay of time and trouble is not what those who take an interest in me would thank me for. They would rather wish me to say what I myself think upon the subject he has opened, and whether there are any points for explanation lying about in the vehement rhetoric he has directed against me. Certainly they will not think there is any call for my assuring them that I am not a hidden sceptic; and I can meet them with the thankful recognition that for a long seventy years, amid mental trials sharp and heavy, I can, in my place and in my measure, adopt the words of St. Polycarp before his martyrdom: "For fourscore years and six I have served my Lord, and He never did me harm, but much good; and can I leave Him now?" But this immunity neither has nor ought to have hindered me from entering with sympathy in what I have written into the anxieties of those who are in this respect less happy than myself; and be it a crime or not, I confess to have tried to aid them according to my ability. Not that I can pretend to be well read in mental science, but I have employed such arguments and views as are congenial to my own mind, and I have not been unsuccessful in my use of them.

As I have said in print: "A man's experiences are enough for himself, but he cannot speak for others. . . . . He brings together his reasons and relies on them, because they are his own, and this is his primary evidence; and he has a second ground of evidence in the testimony of those who agree with him. But his best evidence is in the former, which is derived from his own thoughts. . . . He states what are personally his own grounds in natural and revealed religion, holding them to be so sufficient that he thinks that others also do hold them implicitly or in substance, or would hold them, if they inquired fairly, or will hold if they listen to him, or do not hold from impediments, invincible or not as it may be, into which he has no call to inquire." [*Gram. of Assent*, pp. 385-6.]

§ 39.

The meaning of the word " Reason " continued.

Enough of introduction : I begin with what is of prime importance in Dr. Fairbairn's charges against me—the sense in which I use the word " Reason," against which Reason I have made so many and such strong protests. It is a misleading word, as having various meanings. It is sometimes used to signify the gift which distinguishes man from brute ; I have not so used it. In this sense it is mainly a popular word, not a scientific. When so taken it is not a faculty of the mind, rather it is the mind itself; or it is a generalization; or it stands for the seat of all the mental powers together. For myself, I have taken it to mean the faculty of Reasoning in a large sense, nor do I know what other English word can be used to express that faculty. Besides, " Reason " is of a family of words all expressive of Reasoning. I may add that it is the meaning which Dr. Johnson puts upon the word, and the meaning which he traces through its derivative senses, corroborating his account of it by passages from English authors. " Reason," he says, is " the power by which man deduces one proposition from another, or proceeds from premisses to consequences ; the rational faculty ; discursive power." Also it is the sense, I suppose, which Principal Fairbairn himself gives to the word, for he speaks of " the region of reason and reasoning " (p. 667).

§ 40.

The sense of " Reason " as used in the " Apologia."

This being the recognised sense of the word, it is quite as important for my present purpose to show it to be the sense in which I have myself used " Reason " in what I have written at various times; though Dr. Fairbairn, as having "studied " all my books (p. 663), must be well aware of it already. For instance :

First, I discard the vague popular sense of it as the distinguishing gift of man in contrast with the brute creation. "Sometimes," I say, "it stands for all in which man differs from the brutes; and so it includes in its signification the faculty of distinguishing between right and wrong and the directing principle of conduct. In this sense certainly I do not here use it." (*Univ. Serm.*, p. 58.)

This is but a negative account of it, but in another Sermon I speak more distinctly. "By the exercise of reason is properly meant any process or act of the mind, by which, from knowing one thing, it advances on to know another." (*Ibid*, p. 223.)

Again : "It is obvious that even our senses convey us but a little way out of ourselves, and introduce us to the external world only under circumstances, under conditions of time and place, and of certain media through which they act. We must be near things to touch them; we must be interrupted by no simultaneous sounds in order to hear them; we must have light to see them; we can neither see, hear, nor touch things past or future. Now, Reason is that faculty of the mind by which this deficiency is supplied; by which knowledge of things external to us—of beings, facts, and events—is attained beyond the range of sense; . . . . . . it brings us knowledge, whether clear or uncertain, still knowledge, in whatever degree of perfection, from every side; but, at the same time, with this characteristic, that it obtains it indirectly, not directly, ... on the hypothesis of something else . . . being assumed to be true." (*Ibid*, p. 206.)

And again : " Reason, according to the simplest view of it, is the faculty of gaining knowledge without direct perception, or of ascertaining one thing by means of another. In this way it is able, from small beginnings, to create to itself a world of ideas, which do or do not correspond to the things themselves for which they stand, or are true or not according as it is exercised soundly or otherwise." (Vide *Serm.* xiii, p. 256.)

§ 41.

The result of this use of " Reason."

These passages of mine are on subjects of their own; but they will serve the purpose of making clear the account which in times past, as now, I have given of the reasoning faculty ; and, in doing so, I have implied how great a faculty it is. In

its versatility, its illimitable range, its subtlety, its
power of concentrating many ideas on one point, it
is for the acquisition of knowledge all-important or
rather necessary, with this drawback, however, in
its ordinary use, that in every exercise of it, it
depends for success upon the assumption of prior
acts similar to that which it has itself involved,
and therefore is reliable only conditionally. Its
process is a passing from an antecedent to a consequent, and according as the start so is the issue.
In the province of religion, if it be under the happy
guidance of the moral sense,* and with teachings
which are not only assumptions in form but certainties in fact, it will arrive at indisputable truth, and
then the house is at peace ; but if it be in the hands
of enemies, who are under the delusion that their
arbitrary assumptions are self-evident axioms, the
reasoning will start from false premises, and the
mind will be in a state of melancholy disorder.
But in no case need the reasoning faculty itself be
to blame or responsible, except when identified with
the assumptions of which it is the instrument. I
repeat, it is but an instrument ; as such I have
viewed it, and no one but Dr. Fairbairn would say
as he does—that the bad employment of a faculty
was a "division," a "contradiction," and "a radical
antagonism of nature," and "the death of the
natural proof" of a God. The eyes, and the hands,

---

* Vide *Art*. III, §§ 2 and 4.

and the tongue, are instruments in their very nature. We may speak of a wanton eye, and a murderous hand, and a blaspheming tongue, without denying that they can be used for good purposes as well as for bad.

§ 42.

Its use as recognised by other writers.

Such, in accordance with received English litera- ture, is the sense in which I have used the word "Reason," and not in the sense of foreign writers. It must by no means then be supposed that I think a natural faculty of man to have been revolutionized, because an enemy of truth has availed itself of it for evil purposes. This is what Dr. Fairbairn imputes to me, for I hold, it seems, that "in spite of the conscience there is" not a little "latent atheism in the nature, and especially in the reason, of man" (p. 665). Here he has been misled by the epithets which I attached in the *Apologia* to the Reason, as viewed in its continuous strenuous action against religious truth, both in and outside the Catholic body. I will explain why I did so. I had been referring to the fall of man, and our Cate- chisms tell us that the Fall opened upon him three great spiritual enemies, the World, the Flesh, and the Devil, which need to be resisted by means natural and supernatural. I was led by my general subject to select one of the three for my remarks, and to ask how it acted, and by what instruments? The instruments of the Evil One are best known to himself; the Flesh needs no instruments; the Reasoning Faculty is the instrument of the World. The World is that vast community impregnated by religious error which mocks and rivals the Church by claiming to be its own witness, and to be infallible. Such is the World, the False Prophet (as I called it fifty years ago), and Reasoning is its voice. I had in my mind such Apostolic sayings as "Love not the world, neither the things of the world," and "A friend of the world is the enemy of God;" but I was very loth, as indeed I am also now on the present occasion, to *preach.* Instead then of saying "the World's Reason," I said "Reason actually and historically," "Reason in fact and concretely in fallen man," "Reason in the educated intellect of England, France, and Germany," Reason in "every Government and every civilization through the world which is under the influence of the European mind," Reason in the "wild living intellect of man," which needs (to have) "its stiff neck bent," that ultra "freedom of thought, which is in itself one of the greatest of our natural gifts," "that deep, plausible scepticism" which is "the development of human reason as practically exercised by the natural man." That is, Reason as wielded by the Living World, against the teaching of the Infallible Church.

And I was sanctioned in thus speaking by St. Paul's parallel use of the word "Wisdom," which is one of the highest gifts given to man, and which, nevertheless, he condemns, considered as the World's Wisdom, pronouncing that "the World by Wisdom knew not God."

§ 43.

The sense of "Reason" as superseded and perverted by other writers.

In thus shifting the blame of hostility to religion from man reasoning to man collective, I may seem to be imputing to a divine ordinance (for such human society is) what I have disclaimed to be imputing to man's gift of reason; but this is to mistake my meaning. The World is a collection of individual men, and any one of them may hold and take on himself to profess unchristian doctrine, and do his best to propagate it; but few have the power for such a work, or the opportunity. It is by their union into one body, by the intercourse of man with man and the sympathy thence arising, that error spreads and becomes an authority. Its separate units which make up the body rely upon each other, and upon the whole, for the truth of their assertions; and thus assumptions and false reasonings are received without question as certain truths, on the credit of alternate appeals and mutual cheers and *imprimaturs*.

I should like, if I could, to give a specimen of these assumptions, and the reasonings founded on them, which in my *Apologia* I considered to be "corrosive" of all religion; but before doing so, I must guard against misconstruction of what I am proposing. First, I am not proposing to carry on an argument against Dr. Fairbairn, whose own opinions, to tell the truth, I have not a dream of; but I would gladly explain, or rather complete on particular points, the statements I have before now made in several works about Faith and Reason. Next, I can truly say that, neither in those former writings nor now, have I particular authors in mind who are or are said to be prominent teachers in what I should call the school of the World. Such an undertaking would require a volume, instead of half a dozen pages such as these, and the study too of many hard questions; and I repeat, here I am attempting little more than to fill up a few of the *lacunæ* to be found in a chapter of the *Apologia*, which, like the rest of the book, had to be written *extempore*; certainly I have no intention here of entering into controversy. And further, I wish to call attention to a passage in one of my St. Mary's Sermons, headed, "The World our Enemy," which is not directly on the subject of religious error, but still is applicable when I would fain clear myself in what I am saying of falling unintentionally into any harsh and extreme judgments. A few sentences will be enough to show the drift with which I quote it.

"There is a question," I say, "which it will be well to consider, viz., how far the world is a separate body from the Church of God. The two are certainly contrasted in Scripture, but the Church, so far from being literally and in fact separate from the world, is within it. The Church is a body, gathered together indeed in the world, but only in a process of separation from it. The world's power is over the Church, because the Church has gone forth into the world to save the world. All Christians are in the world and of the world, so far as Evil still has dominion over them, and not even the best of us is clean every whit from sin. Though then, in our idea of the one and the other, and in their principles and in their future prospects, the Church is one thing and the World is another, yet in present matter of fact the Church is of the World, not separate from it; for the grace of God has but partial possession even of religious men, and the best that can be said of us is that we have two sides, a light side and a dark, and that the dark happens to be the outermost. Thus we form part of the world to each other, though we be not *of* the world. Even supposing there were a society of men influenced individually by Christian motives, still, this society, viewed as a whole, would be a worldly one; I mean a society holding and maintaining many errors, and countenancing many bad practices. Evil ever floats on the top" (*Sermons*, vol. vii, p. 35-36). In accordance with these cautions I will here avow that good men may imbibe to their great disadvantage the spirit of the world, and, on the contrary, inferior men may keep themselves comparatively clear of it.

§ 44.

Illustrations in point.

These explanations being made, I take up the serious protest which I began in the *Apologia*. I say then that if, as I believe, the world, which the Apostles speak of so severely as a False Prophet,* is identical with what we call human Society now, then there never was a time since Christianity was, when, together with the superabundant temporal advantages which by it may come to us, it had the opportunity of being a worse enemy to religion and religious truth than it is likely to be in the years now opening upon mankind. I say so, because in its width and breadth it is so much better educated and informed than it ever was before, and because of its extent, so multiform and almost ubiquitous. Its conquests in the field of physical science, and its intercommunion of place with place, are a source to

---

* Vide *University Sermons*, "Contrast between Faith and Sight."

it both of pride and of enthusiasm. It has triumphed over time and space; knowledge it has proved to be emphatically power; no problems of the universe—material, moral, or religious—are too great for its ambitious essay and its high will to master. There is one obstacle in its path, I mean the province of religion. But can religion hope to be successful? It is thought to be already giving way before the presence of what the world considers a new era in the history of man.

§ 45.

As proved in argument.

With these thoughts in my mind, I understand how it has come to pass, what has struck me as remarkable, that the partizans and spokesmen of Society, when they come to the question of religion, seem to care so little about proving what they maintain, and, on the warrant of their philosophy, are content silently and serenely to take by implication their first principles for granted, as if, like the teachers of Christianity, they were inspired and infallible. To the World, indeed, its own principles are infallible, and need no proof. Now if its representatives would but be candid, and say that their assumptions, as ours, are infallible, we should know where they stand; there would be an end of controversy. As I have said before now, "Half the

G

controversies in the world, could they be brought to a plain issue, would be brought to a prompt termination. Parties engaged in them would then perceive . . . that in substance . . . their difference was of first principles. . . . When men understand what each other means, they see for the most part that controversy is either superfluous or hopeless " (*Univ. Serm.*, p. 200-1). The World, then, has its first principles of religion, and so have we. If this were understood, I should not have any present cause of protest against its Reason as corrosive of our faith. I do not grudge the World its gods, its principles, and its worship; but I protest against its şending them into Christian lecture rooms, libraries, societies, and companies, as if they were Christian—criticising, modelling, measuring, altering, improving, as it thinks, our doctrines, principles, and methods of thought, which we refer to divine informants. One of my *University Sermons*, in 1831, is on this subject; it is called "The Usurpations of Reason," and I have nothing to change in the substance of it. I was very jealous of "the British Association " at its commencement, not as if science were not a divine gift, but because its first members seemed to begin with a profession of Theism, when I said their business was to keep to their own range of subjects. I argued that if they began with Theism, they would end with Atheism. At the end of half a century I have still more reason to be suspicious of the upshot of secular schools. Not, of course, that I suppose that the flood of unbelief will pour over us in its fulness at once. A large inundation requires a sufficient time, and there are always in the worst times witnesses for the Truth to stay the plague.* Above all things there is the Infallible Church, of which I spoke so much in the *Apologia.* With this remark I am led on to another subject.

§ 46.

Its bearing on dogmatic fact.

I will take an illustration of the prospect before us in the instance of a doctrine which is more than most the subject of dispute just now. Lest I should be mistaken, I avow myself, while holding it, to do so, not because of the disintegrating consequences of letting it go, but on the simple word of the Divine Informant; yet I want to show the prospective development of error where Faith is not. A hundred years ago the God of Christianity was called a God of mere benevolence. That could not long be maintained, first, because He was the God of the Old Testament as well as of the New, and next and specially because the New Testament opened upon us the Woe thrice uttered by the Judge himself, the Woe

---

* Vide one of my *University Sermons,* " Personal Influence the means of propagating the Truth."

unquenchable which is denounced upon transgressors.*
But the instinct of modern civilization denies the
very idea of such a doom in the face of a progressive
future. As to the Old Testament, it has been
comparatively easy to loosen its connection with
Christianity; but how shall we release ourselves
from the strong unequivocal teaching of the New?
And, before we consider it, let me ask, is there
nothing in the history of mankind to bring home to
us that there exists a world of evil as well as a world
of good? Is there not now—has there not ever
been—a vast aggregate of sin and suffering, of intense
weary pain, bodily and mental, of wicked self-con-
suming passions and their widespread destructiveness,
occupying the earth for an unknown succession of
centuries? Consider only the long pain and anguish,
which are the ordinary accompaniments of death.
Supposing mankind to have lasted many thousand
years, the suffering has been just as long; there has
been no interval of rest.

This for the past and present; but you will say
that to each who suffers here suffering has an
end and is comparatively brief, and that this is
not a difficulty to be compared to that of suffering
which is to be for ever, and that you cannot receive
the teaching of Scripture, if the word "eternal"
there used of future punishment must be taken to
mean everlasting:—Indeed? would you really then

---

* Vide *S. Marc*, ix, 43, 45, 47, Vulg.

be content if such an interpretation of the word "eternal" as you desire were conceded to you? Do you want nothing more? What is the nature of the punishment as defined in Scripture? Fire. You will say this is a figure of speech; even granting it, still, figures are representations of fact, and must not be explained away. Besides, Dives speaks of "torments," and more than once or twice we read of "wailing and gnashing of teeth." This being considered, what time do you contemplate as being represented by the word "eternal?" an æon? a thousand years? I do not believe it—you would not be satisfied, though the period was contracted to a hundred, nay to fifty, or to twenty, or to a dozen; not satisfied, though it be granted, or rather explained, that the degrees of punishment are numberless. In spite of the word of Scripture, your imagination would carry you away; it is a subject beyond you; it is not duration that is your supreme difficulty, rather it is pain. We have no positive notion of suffering in relation to simple duration. Time and eternity are not qualities of suffering; nor is punishment *therefore* infinite, because it is without end. What we know about the eternal state is negative, that there is no future when it will not be. All that is necessary for us to be told is that the state of good and evil is irreversible. We know there will be a judgment and a final decision. "After death, judgment," and before it a trial in order to it. Such a dispensation of things is revealed as definite, as once for all. If this, too, is denied, as it probably will be, then another Christian doctrine goes.

§ 47.

Digressions in consequence.

But again, the Scripture announcement of the Last Judgment may be viewed in another aspect:— what do we know of the obstacles to a reconciliation between God and man? Suppose the punishment is self-inflicted; suppose it is the will, the proud determination of the lost to breathe defiance to his Maker, or the utter loathing of His Presence or His Court, which makes a reconciliation with Him impossible. To change such a one may be to destroy his identity. Moreover, what do we know of the rules necessary for the moral government of the universe? What acts of judgment are or are not compatible or accordant with the bearing of a Just Judge? and by what self-evident process do we ascertain this? What of His knowledge who is able to "search the heart?" We are told He is one who "overcomes when He is judged;" ought we not to have the whole case spread out for us, as it will be at the Last Day, before we venture to pronounce upon its details? they are parts of a whole. Go to what is the root of the mystery, and tell us what is the Origin of Evil. Solve this, and you may see your way to dispose of other difficulties. Does not this greatest of mysteries, the " Origin and prevalence of Evil," fall as heavily upon Natural Religion as future punishment upon Revelation ? After all, the Theist needs Faith as well as the Christian. All religion has its mysteries, and all mysteries are correlative with faith ; and, where faith is absent, the action of relentless "reason," under the assumptions of educated society, passes on (as I have given offence by asserting) from Catholicity to Theism, and from Theism to a materialistic cause of all things. Dr. Fairbairn calls it sceptical to preach Faith, and to practise it.

§ 48.

" The Atonement " or " Divine Reconciliation."

I have confined myself to the Divine Judgment; but this is only one of the doctrines which the abolition of the Woe to come is made to compromise. Here again modern philosophy acts to the injury of religion, natural and revealed. Those solemn warnings of Scripture against disobedience to the law of right and wrong are but fellows of the upbraidings and menaces of the human Conscience. The belief in future punishment will not pass away without grave prejudice to that high Monitor. Are you, in weakening its warning voice, to lose an ever-present reminder of an Unseen God ? It is a bad time to lose that voice when efforts so serious have so long been making to resolve it into some intellectual principle or secular motive. But there is another doctrine, too, that suffers when future punishment is tampered with, namely, what is commonly called the "Atonement." The Divine Victim took the place of man : how will this doctrine stand, if the final doom of the wicked is denied? Every one who escapes the penalty of pain, escapes it by virtue of the Atonement made instead of it; but so great a price as was paid for the remission supposes an unimaginable debt. If the need was not immense, would such a Sacrifice have been called for? Does not that Sacrifice throw a fearful light upon the need of it? And if the need be denied, will not the Sacrifice be unintelligible? The early martyrs give us their sense of it; they considered their torments as a deliverance from their full deserts, and felt that, had they recanted, it would have been at the risk of their eternal welfare. The Great Apostle is in his writings full of gratitude to the Power who has "delivered us from the wrath to come." It is a foundation of the whole spiritual fabric on which his life is built. What remains of his Christianity if he is no longer to be penetrated by the thought of that second death from which he had been now delivered? Further, what becomes of the doctrine of the Incarnation? Can the religion with which Society at present threatens us be the same as the Apostle's, if these solemn doctrines are in this Religion and not in that?

§ 49.

The need of dogma.

Shall I be answered that it is only dogma that is left out in modern Christianity? I understand; dogma is unnecessary for faith, because faith is but a sentiment; vicarious suffering is an injustice; spiritual benefits cannot be wrought by material instruments; sin is but a weakness or an ignorance; this life has nearer claims on us than the next; the nature of man is sufficient for itself; the rule of law admits no miracles; and so on. There is any number of these assumptions ready for the nonce, and there is Micio's axiom in the Play, soon, perhaps, to come upon us, "Non est flagitium, mihi crede, adolescentulum scortari." When Reason starts from assumptions such as these, its corrosive quality ought to be sufficient to satisfy Dr. Fairbairn.

This is all I think it necessary to set down in explanation of passages in my *Apologia*. As to my other writings, I can safely leave them to take care of themselves. Anyone that looks into them will see how strangely Principal Fairbairn has misrepresented them.

———

N.B.—*The paging, in quotations made, as above, from "The Contemporary Review," May, 1885, follows the paging of that work, viz., pp. 665, 667.*

☞ *The following Sections are appended to the Article from " The Contemporary Review."*

§ 50.

On Philosophical Scepticism.

Principal Fairbairn, in his Article in the *Contemporary* of December, 1885, as an answer to my explanation in October, has repeated his charges against me with much vehemence, but, as I hope to show, with small success. He still considers me as thinking and writing on a foundation of " underlying scepticism: " he calls it however philosophical scepticism, by which I understand him to mean a sort of scepticism which I am not aware of myself ; at least I can only suppose that he contrasts philosophical with personal. Though I do not understand the distinction, I am glad to receive from him a token of good feeling and courtesy such as I believe this to be.

He says that I am only a philosophic sceptic, and that he has taken considerable pains to bring this home to me. He says, " What he [the Cardinal] was charged with, and in terms so careful and guarded as ought to have excluded all possible misconceptions, was 'metaphysical or philosophical' scepticism." This sort of scepticism he proceeds to define, but I fear I cannot call him happy in his attempt. He defines it as "a system which . . . subjectively affirms the impotence of human reason for the discovery of truth."* Such a definition (in religious questions, as in the case before us) is seriously incomplete. If it be taken in its letter, I certainly cannot deny that it has proved me to be a sceptic, for I do affirm the impotence of human reason for the discovery of a great many truths; but then it has done so at the expense of convicting of scepticism all Catholics, besides all theologians of the Greek Church and all orthodox Anglicans. Dr. Fairbairn's definition tells against all whosoever hold on faith the great truths of Revelation, such as the Holy Trinity and the Incarnation, and beyond all mistake includes in its imputation the Vatican Council itself, which expressly anathematises any one who shall say "that in Divine Revelation there are contained no true and properly so called mysteries, but that all the dogmas of faith can be understood and demonstrated from natural principles by means of Reason properly cultivated." If to deny the omnipotence of reason in the discovery of truth is scepticism, I am in good company.

---

* Dr. Fairbairn's words are, "Scepticism in philosophy means a system which affirms either subjectively, the impotence of the reason for the discovery of the truth, or objectively, the inaccessibility of truth to the reason."

Let me take a more exact and adequate definition of scepticism, and see if I fall under it. The definition of scepticism to which I am myself accustomed is such as this: "Scepticism is the system which holds that no certainty is attainable, as not in other things so not in questions of religious truth and error." How have I incurred this reproach? On the contrary, I have not only asserted, with a strength of words which has sometimes incurred censure, my belief in religious truth, but have insisted on the certainty of such truth, and on Certitude as having a place among the constituents of human thought;—analysing it, discriminating it, and giving tests of it, with a direct apprehension and manipulation quite incompatible with my never asking myself whether intellectually I was in any sense a sceptic or not. It seems to me that the charge of scepticism which has been used against me elsewhere, as well as in England, is a mere idle word, serviceable in an intellectual combat; and I think it would be more charitable in opponents if, instead of imputing it to any dissatisfaction which I have at any time expressed with certain arguments used in Catholic controversy, they ascribed it, not to an underlying scepticism as to the truths in dispute, but rather to an unmeasured and even reckless confidence in them, or, again, to an attempt to test the availableness at the present time of certain conventional proofs used for polemical purposes.

§ 51.

On the Meaning of the word " Reason."

So much on Dr. Fairbairn's definition of what he considers the "philosophical" scepticism which runs through all my writings. And now I come to what seems to him a main instance of it—my account of Reason considered as the faculty of reasoning. Here he drops his unfortunate attempt at defining; at least he does not tell us what Reason is, as far as I can make out, but he is severe in pronouncing it to be constitutive, architectonic, true, and religious; whereas, in my idea of it, it is a mere instrument, " an inferential instrument," from which nothing great can come. He says, " What works as a mere instrument never handles what it works in, the things remain outside it, and have no place or standing within its being . . . To a reason without religious character . . . . truth is inaccessible. . . This is philosophical scepticism." I am quite ready to meet him on this new ground of argument. He says that Reason, as I consider it, is necessarily sceptical; let us see.

Here, first, I must protest against its being magisterially ruled by Dr. Fairbairn that the word Reason has one and one only definite scientific meaning, accepted by all authorities in metaphysics, and incapable of any other ; whereas, before coming to the question of particular words and phrases, I really wish it settled whether there is a recognised science of metaphysics at all. Certainly in 1831 and the following years the terminology which he takes for granted was little known in Oxford,* nor indeed any terminology but Aristotle's; much less were any words or definitions taken for stereotyped truths. I have no great remorse that for fifty years I have used my native tongue as a vehicle for religious and ethical discussions; in this instance, indeed, with the sanction of a writer who is commonly called *par excellence* our lexicographer. Provided I am careful to record the senses in which I use words, it is not the part of a fair critic to take them in another sense, and in that sense to be tragic in his reprobation of them. My turn of mind has never led me towards metaphysics; rather it has been logical, ethical, practical. As to the word "Reason," it would have been a strange digression had I, in speaking of the religious state of Europe, entered into an account of the faculties of the human mind and the analysis which has been made of them by various metaphysicians.

Here it is very pertinent to quote in my favour the remarks of Sir William Hamilton; they will protect me in the acts of private judgment which are so offensive to Dr. Fairbairn.

"'Reason,'" he says, "is a very vague, vacillating, and equivocal word. . . . . Throwing aside its

---

* I am not forgetful of Mr. Johnson's translation of Tennemann, in 1832, but I doubt if it was much read.

employment in most languages for *cause, motive, argument,* &c., considering it only as a philosophical word, denoting a faculty or complement of faculties, in this relation it is found employed in the following meanings, not only by different individuals, but frequently to a greater or less extent by the same philosopher. . . . . Nothing can be more vague and various than his [Kant's] employment of the word [Reason] . . . . but even in his [Kant's] abusive employment of the term, ... no consistency was maintained." (*Hamilton on Reid,* Note A, § v. 7.)

In this latitude and confusion of the terminology found among professed metaphysicians I think I have a right to my own way of regarding the faculty of Reason, whether I fail in it or not; and that the more because, while I am following the English use of the word, it is a personal satisfaction to me to be able also to believe that I am adhering to the ecclesiastical. At least Gregory the 16th, Pius the 9th, and the Vatican Council, when they would speak of " proving " and of " demonstrating," refer the act of the mind to " human reason."*

---

* Gregor. XVI. In causa Bautain, 1840 : " Ratio cum certitudine authenticitatem Revelationis *probat.*" Pius Encyc., 1846 : "*Recta* ratio fidei veritatem *demonstrat.*" Concil. Vatican., 1870 : "*Recta* ratio fidei fundamenta *demon-strat.*" And it speaks of "argumenta humanæ rationis." The "lumen rationis" I will notice presently. Vide also contrast between antecedent opinion and pre-existent truth in my *University Sermons.*

§ 52.

On the Faculty of Reason.

When, then, in times past I have wished to express my anxiety lest serious dangers might be in store for educated society, my first business was to determine what sense I ought to give to the word "Reason," claimed by Rationalists as if specially belonging to themselves. The only senses of it which I knew—nay, which I know of it now—are two: in one of the two senses it seems to be a synonyme for "Mind," as used in contrast with the condition of brutes. This is far too broad an account of it to be of service in such a purpose as my own, and in consequence I have been thrown of necessity on the sense which is its alternative, viz., that reason is the faculty of reasoning; and though such a view of it does not suggest that venerable and sovereign idea which we usually attach to "Reason," still, as I was not writing metaphysics, but with an ethical and social view, I did not find any great inconvenience in taking the word in its popular, etymological, and, as I hope, ecclesiastical acceptation.

To such a view of Reason however Dr. Fairbairn objects, as leading to scepticism; but I have never thought, as he supposes, of leaving truth to so untrustworthy a protection as reasoning by itself would be to it. The mind without any doubt is made for truth. Still, it does not therefore follow that truth is its object in all its powers. The imagination is a wonderful faculty in the cause of truth, but it often subserves the purposes of error—so do our most innocent affections. Every faculty has its place. There is a faculty in the mind which acts as a complement to reasoning, and as having truth for its direct object thereby secures its use for rightful purposes. This faculty, viewed in its relation to religion, is, as I have before said, the moral sense; but it has a wider subject-matter than religion, and a more comprehensive office and scope, as being "the apprehension of first principles," and Aristotle has taught me to call it νοῦς, or the *noetic* faculty.*

§ 53.

On the Action of Reason as determined and regulated by other Faculties.

How this faculty of νοῦς bears upon the action of reasoning scarcely requires many words. I have considered Reasoning as an instrument—that is, an instrument for the use of other faculties, for who ever heard of an instrument without there being, as I have taken for granted, some distinct power to make use of it? Now to know what the reasoning faculty needs for the purposes of religion we must consider it, not in its abstract idea, but in the

---

* ἐπιστήμη, Aristotle's second faculty, conversant with necessary truth, answers well (ana- logically) to Reason, as I am considering it. (Vide Chase on Aristotle's ἐπιστήμη, p. 201.)

H

concrete. When so viewed, it includes an antecedent and a consequent, and it is at once plain what is the connecting link between it and (for instance) the noetic faculty. The antecedent of the reasoning is that link; for the matter (as it is called) of the antecedent belongs both to the reasoning and also to those other faculties, many or few, which have for their object the antecedent.* Great faculty as reasoning certainly is, it is from its very nature in all subjects dependent upon other faculties. It receives from them the antecedent with which its action starts; and when this antecedent is true, there is no longer in religious matters room for any accusation against it of scepticism. In such matters the independent faculty which is mainly necessary for its healthy working and the ultimate warrant of the reasoning act, I have hitherto spoken of as the moral sense; but, as I have already said, it has a wider subject-matter than religion, and a larger name than moral sense, as including intuitions, and this is what Aristotle calls νοῦς.

---

* *E.g.*, we may *hope* for a revelation by reason of the *divine goodness.* Here the "hope," which is the consequent of the reasoning, is arrived at by the antecedent the "divine goodness," which antecedent not only belongs to the reasoning but to the faculty of theology also, being a truth belonging to its subject-matter. To put it otherwise, (1) the *hope* of a revelation (2) depends on the *divine goodness*, (3) and the divine goodness depends on theology, therefore the reasoning is regulated by theology.

Here I am struck by what I must call the aridity of Dr. Fairbairn's polemic. What could be more natural, what more congruous, than that there should be a faculty which was concerned with the antecedent of the reasoning, as the reasoning itself is concerned with the consequent, so that the two faculties unite in a joint act, each of the two having need of the other? But instead of accepting this division and arrangement of work, Dr. Fairbairn, I must insist, ungraciously refuses to see a harmony in such an association of two great faculties, and makes them enemies and rivals, as if I inordinately exalted the moral sense and crushed the reason.

I have been speaking of antecedents which are true; other antecedents may be founded on error. Dr. Fairbairn speaks as if the fact that the faculty of reason can be exercised on false antecedents as well as on true, opens a way to scepticism. That depends on what is meant by reason; my own account of the faculty may be wrong, but at least it has no such tendency. If it has, then all I need say is that since writers in general speak of a right and a wrong use of reason, Dr. Fairbairn, I suppose, would consider them sceptics too. Still, what else can a man mean by speaking of a right use but that there is a wrong?—right, because its antecedents are chosen rightly by the divinely enlightened mind, being such as intuitions, dictates of conscience, the inspired Word, the decisions of the Church, and the like; whereas we call it false reason or sophistry when its antecedents are determined by pride, self-trust, unbelief, human affection, narrow self-interest, bad education, or other mental agencies, which are found in the world and in the individual. It corroborates my doctrine of these two aspects of reason that, as if with the same drift of marking the broad difference between one aspect of the reasoning faculty and the other, ecclesiastical treatises speak of the "*lumen* rationis," as they speak of the "*recta ratio*," as if there was a use of reason which was really darkness.

§ 54.

On the Mind's Faculties existing, not "re," but "ratione,"
and therefore only abstract names for its operations.

I have tried in the above pages, as in my original article, to explain with all necessary precision and clearness what I understand, whether rightly or wrongly, by the faculty of Reason, and what is the office which I attribute to it. I wonder whether it is a fault of mine that I do not find myself able to discern a like frankness on the part of Principal Fairbairn. Perhaps if he had informed me what he meant by "Reason," as I have myself freely expressed my own account of it, it would be easier to me to understand his logic; but he seems to me to heap up epithets of praise upon what he calls Reason without telling us what Reason is In this he is unfair to himself; for how can a disputant hope to recommend to others what he has not yet himself taken the pains to master? I will give a few instances out of many of this mistake in him.

He arrays against me a sufficient number of *dicta*, which in their form seem to be meant for axioms, but which I must call unintelligible. Here are specimens of them:

1. "The reasoning process, to be valid, must proceed from principles valid to the *reason*." In what sense does he here use the word Reason? Does he mean the reasoning faculty or the noetic?— though as an argument against me it does not matter to me which. If he means the reasoning, I do not admit what is simply an assumption; if the noetic, since in that case I agree with him, it does me no harm.

2. "To use principles truly, one must be able to judge concerning their truth." Certainly; just as to use scientific terms rightly we must first give their definitions; but we judge of the truth of principles by the appropriate faculty, and not by a faculty which is not concerned with them. We cannot speak of Reason — that is, Reasoning — as *judging* truth; it does but *treat* of it. The judgment lies in the antecedent, and in the particular faculty to which the antecedent belongs.

3. "How can Reason truly and justly act, even as a mere instrument of inference, on the basis of premisses which it neither found, nor framed, nor

verified, being indeed so constituted as not to be able to do any one of these things?" How? By looking for means of doing so in the right direction. There cannot be an act of reasoning without an antecedent, and to determine the antecedent we must use the particular faculty to which the antecedent's subject-matter belongs. In questions of religion it is mainly the noetic, sometimes another; in mathematics, the noetic faculty only. That particular faculty would be able to "find, frame, and verify," which was "so constituted" as to be able " to do any one of these things." Why will Dr. Fairbairn persist in proving that the reasoning faculty cannot do its own work because it cannot do the work of another faculty?

4. Here is another instance of Dr. Fairbairn's finding it easier to attack my account of " Reason" than to state his own. He says I make it "a deductive instrument, void of God, and never able to know Him directly or for itself," p. 850. The answer to this depends upon what he means by Reason: it is the same fallacy all through. He argues with two contrary views of Reason in his hands at the same time, and uses one of them to refute the other. But this is not all; he speaks as if faculties were something real and substantive; whereas they are no more than simple powers. Void of God—that is, I suppose, of religion! Why every faculty may be said to be void of the objects of every other faculty: imagination is void of

memory, memory of sense, and so on. A faculty is as little capable of being "emptied" and made "void" as the act of reading or writing. It is the exercise of a power of the mind itself, and that *pro re nata*; and, when the mind ceases to use it, we may almost say that it is nowhere. Of course, for convenience, we speak of the mind as possessing faculties instead of saying that it acts in a certain way and on a definite subject-matter; but we must not turn a figure of speech into a fact.

§ 55.

On Final Causes.

I consider I have said enough to show that whatever criticisms may fairly be made on the view I have taken of the faculty of reason, they do not bear out Dr. Fairbairn's charge that the view itself is in its nature sceptical, and is used by me with a purpose. But he has a more serious charge in store, very different from anything that has gone before, to which I must now call attention; it is that in this same sceptical spirit I weaken the force of arguments for religion, pronouncing (for instance) that atheism is an hypothesis equally consistent with the phenomena of the physical universe as the hypothesis of a creative intelligence. And, further still, though it is not a subject that I have now immediately before me, that I have wished by such depreciation of the arguments for religion to magnify the teaching of the Catholic Church. I observe as follows:

(1.) From the time that I began to occupy my mind with theological subjects I have been troubled at the prospect, which I considered to lie before us, of an intellectual movement against religion, so special as to have a claim upon the attention of all educated Christians. As early as 1826 I wrote, "As the principles of science are in process of time more fully developed, and become more independent of the religious system, there is much danger lest the philosophical school should be found to separate from the Christian Church, and at length disown the parent to whom it has been so greatly indebted. And this evil has in a measure befallen us," &c., &c. (*Univ. Serm.*, p. 14). This grave apprehension led me to consider the evidences, as they are called, of Religion generally, and the intellectual theory on which they are based. This I attempted with the purpose, as far as lay in my power, not certainly of starting doubts about religion, but of testing and perfecting the proofs in its behalf. In literal warfare, weapons are tested before they are brought into use, and the men are not called traitors who test them. I am far indeed from being satisfied with my own performances; in my *Apologia* I call them tentative. They might be rash, but they were not sceptical, nor had I in my mind any thought, when thus engaged, of substituting for Christian evidences the word of the "Infallible Church," which appears to be Dr. Fairbairn's strange imagination.

(2.) Thus I was brought to the popular argument for a Creator drawn from the marks of what is commonly called Design in the physical world. Led on by Lord Bacon, I found I could not give it that high place among the arguments for religion which is almost instinctively accorded to it by a religious mind. Such a mind starts with an assumption which a man who is not religious requires in the first instance to be proved. A believer in God recognises at once, and justly recognises, the marks of design which are innumerable in the structure of the universe, and has his faith and love invigorated and enlarged by the sight of so minute and tender a Providence. But how is an objector to be met who insists that the problem before us is, when viewed in itself, simply which of two hypotheses is the best key to the phenomena of nature—a system founded on cause and effect, or one founded on a purpose and its fulfilment? It is a controversial question,—not as to what is true to hold, but as to what is safe to maintain. Many things are true in fact which cannot be maintained in argument. What is true to one man is not always true to another. Final causes, says Lord Bacon, " are properly alleged in metaphysics; but in physics are impertinent, and as *remoras* to the ship, that hinder the sciences from holding on their course of improvement, and as introducing a neglect of searching after physical causes."* (Vide my *Idea of a University*, p. 222.) Was Bacon an infidel or a sceptic?

(3.) Another point may be urged against Dr. Fairbairn. He argues as if the finding difficulty in the argument from final causes is to be sceptical to the full extent of invalidating the proofs of the being of a God gained from the existence of physical nature. This is far from being the fact; those proofs are not at all affected by any difficulty which may attach to the argument from final causes. The very fact of the universe is quite independent of final causes, and leads to the recognition of a First Cause. Again, it must be recollected that the argument from Design remains, in the large sense of design, as forcible as ever, even though Final Causes are not included in the sense of the word. I will quote a passage to this effect of my own: "Did we see flint celts, in their various receptacles all over Europe, scored always with certain special and characteristic marks, even though those marks had no assignable meaning or final cause whatever, we should take that very repetition, which indeed is the principle of order, to be a proof of intelligence. The agency, then, which has kept up and keeps up the general laws of nature, energising at once in Sirius and on earth,

---

* *De Augment.*, 5.

and on the earth in its primary period as well as in the nineteenth century, must be Mind, and nothing else, and Mind at least as wide and as enduring in its living action as the immeasurable ages and spaces of the universe on which that agency has left its traces. (Vide *The Grammar of Assent*, p. 72.)

This passage Dr. J. W. Ogle has introduced into his learned *Harveian Oration* of 1880, p. 161, where he also quotes from a letter of mine—1. "By design in Creation is generally meant the application of definite means for the attainment of a definite end, or the aim at a final cause. There is a difficulty I consider, in accepting, in this sense, the 'argument from design' as a strictly logical proof of a creative Mind in the universe." 2. "But design also means *order*, as when we speak of beautiful *designs*, in decorative patterns, in architecture, mosaic, needlework, &c. In this sense of *order*, Design is in every part of the universe, and a proof of an intelligent mind."

And now, if I come to an abrupt conclusion, it is because I have said all that I have felt it a duty to say in answer to Dr. Fairbairn's criticisms. Perhaps I should not have noticed them at all, had I known that I was to have the advantage of Dr. Barry's able, and, as I consider, successful defence of me, last November, though he has taken a larger field for remark than I have felt reason to do.

J. H. N.

www.ingramcontent.com/pod-product-compliance
Lightning Source LLC
Chambersburg PA
CBHW032111010726
47493CB00008B/2542